Nothing could have prepared Nicole Redman for the brutal murder of her six-year old daughter.

Through a cloud of shock and pain, she seeks her daughter's murderer in a world filled with sleazy strip clubs, after-hour joints, and a notorious outlaw biker gang.

She is quickly drawn into a life of illicit sex, drugs, and onto the path of a sadistic hitman.

The Wee Hours

THE WEE HOURS

W.D. BURNS

Mega House Publications

BAD ASS OUTLAW PUBLICATIONS
4216 Riverview Lane
Lorian, OH 44055
www.badassoutlawpublications.com

This book is an original publication of Bad Ass Outlaw Publications.

William Daniel Burns
THE WEE HOURS
Library of Congress
Copyright 2010
TXu001692272
revised 2015

Editing, typesetting and cover design by J.D. Williams
(www.behance.net/jdwilliams)

ISBN: 978-0-9962651-0-2

Printed in The United States of America

10 9 8 7 6 5 4 3 2 1

THE WEE HOURS

INDEX

Dedication

To my beautiful wife, Bonnie. For without her I would have never known the meaning of true love.

Acknowledgements

Special thanks to Colleen Brown, for without her assistance this book would not have been possible. Props to my Editor in Cheif and friend, Ronnie Jones.

IN THE BEGINNING...

Nicole Scott was raised in the small country town of Adel, Georgia. There was a three year difference between Nicole and her younger sister. Her father Alton Scott was an avid sportsman with aspirations of having a son. At a young age, Nicole captured his heart , spending most of her time being the perfect Tomboy. Nicole was not afraid to get her hands dirty, and by the age of ten he had taught her to fish, hunt, and survive in the woods. She was fearless in the face of any adventure he took her on.

Alton Scott died from a heart attack when Nicole was twelve.

Nicole cursed God and cried for weeks.

Nicole was fifteen when she met Charlie Redman in high school. Charlie was tall and personable, his being known as a bad boy fascinated the young and impressionable Nicole. A romance followed, which did not sit well with Nicole's mother. In her eyes, Charlie Redman was a no account, good for nothing, pot smoking hippy. The more her mother disliked Charlie, the more Nicole came to adore him. She was sixteen when she broke the news to her mother that she was pregnant. Charlie proposed and they were quickly married by the local Justice of the Peace.

With a family to support, Charlie moved them to Baltimore, Maryland, where he felt there were better job opportunities.

When Charlie went to prison, he was the second man who had left her alone. But this time she was left with a daughter to support.

CHAPTER ONE
A MOTHER's LOVE

Just outside of Baltimore, Maryland, lies the town of Glen Burnie. Five miles from there is the quiet suburban community of Blossom Hills. Nicole Redman had recently divorced and moved from the City to a home at 108 Dupont Avenue. Her ex-husband had served time in prison, and she desperately wanted to provide her daughter a better life. Presently, Nicole was busy tending her flower garden in front of the house, while her six year old daughter, Charlotte Lynn, played in the middle of the street. There were no sidewalks in the small community, all of the lawns running up to the edge of the curb, making it a custom for the neighborhood children to play right out in the road.

Wearing a yellow sun-dress and brown sandals, she hummed softly to herself, patiently marking the street in white chalk, in preparation for a game of hopscotch. Her happy big brown eyes shining like the sun, her long brown pigtail flopping with her every twist and turn. Already the beautiful little girl was the darling of the block, her sweet laughter following her wherever she went. Like most times, there was very little motor traffic, and the neighbors watched carefully for children riding bicycles, roller staking, or playing in the street. After marking the street, Charlotte picked up a stone and tossed it into one of the squares.

"One potato, two potato, three potato, four..."

Charlotte bent over, picked up the stone and tossed it again before continuing her count.

The sudden sound of screeching tires and a racing engine broke through the serenity of playing children. Nicole snapped her head up at the sound of the speeding car.

"Charlotte! Charlotte," she screamed at the top of her lungs, a look of horror crossing her face.

Charlotte never saw the speeding car as it shot over the hilly street. The car crushed the small girl like a grape, sending blood and gore across the paved street, her yellow dress no longer recognizable as a garment worn by a child.

Up and down the block people cried out in shocked horror, some of them running forward to rush their under aged children inside the protection of their homes. One father was so sickened by what he witnessed that he lost his breakfast in his driveway. The car turned left at the first cross street, never slowing, quickly vanishing. Little Charlotte lay in a pool of blood, with streams of blood filling the cracks of the street.

A neighbor ran out of his house yelling to his wife, "Call the police!" He knew, like everyone looking on knew, Charlotte was dead.

"Why? Oh God, Why?" Nicole cried her anguish, looking to the heavens for an answer.

"What kind of person could hit a child and just keep on going." One of the onlookers asked, the sound of emergency vehicles suddenly sounding in the back ground.

By the time the police and paramedics arrived on the scene, two male neighbors had forcibly removed Nicole from the blood soaked remains of her daughter. She was crying and screaming while covered in blood.

"I saw it all," a male neighbor was quick to declare to the first officers to arrive."The driver was a white male, with brown hair, and possibly in his thirties. The car was an older grayish-blue Pontiac Bonneville. He must've been doing fifty miles an hour when he flew over the hill. I don't know how he managed to make that turn."

It was a full ten minutes before a Detective of homicide showed up from the Anne Arundel County Sheriff's Department. Even though Detective David Allen Hill was a Sergeant with a world of experience, he was shocked by the scattered remains of the little girl. He immediately ordered the entire street cordoned off and the spectators pushed back to a respectful distance. He quickly had a group of ten uniformed officers going door to door in search of witnesses, and several more questioning those standing in the gathering crowd. When he soon discovered that the little girl named Charlotte was only six years old, he grew even more angry and determined to find the person responsible.

Detective Hill next went into the house of the victim to speak with her mother, but was quickly informed that the mother was being treated for shock by paramedics, and it would be some time before she could be questioned. Instead he went back outside in search of the other two Detectives who would be working the case under him. There was Robert 'Bob' Bratten and Charlie Aburn, both of them Detectives with plenty of experience in cases like this. He found them both down the block questioning the neighbor who earlier had thrown up his breakfast in his own driveway.

"Did anyone get the license plate number," he asked them the second they finished with the neighbor. It was a routine question, and he got the answer he was anticipating.

"No such luck," Charlie answered.

"Sarge, the Bonneville was found a mile away from here in an I.G.A. parking lot on Fort Smallwood road. It's being dusted for fingerprints," Bob offered.

"Call the Fire Department. I want a truck out here to hose down the street," Sergeant Hill ordered. It was senseless scenes like this that made his blood boil. He would like to beat the shit out of the son of a bitch that did this.

It was another half an hour before he could get in to speak with the mother of the deceased child. When he first saw her, she was seated on a living room sofa with tears streaming from her hazel eyes. He glanced briefly around the small living room, taking careful note of the cleanliness of the room. He was pleased to see how neat and orderly Nicole Redman kept her home. It told him a great deal about the woman in question.

"Mrs. Redman," Hill spoke quietly.

"My baby...my baby!" Nicole repeated, over and over, tears streaming down her cheeks.

Detective Hill looked down on her in sadness. "If you can I need to ask you a few questions."

"Miss."

She spoke absently. "What do you want?"

"Did you see who did this?"

"All I saw was my baby getting run over by a speeding car," she cried. "The bastard! I hope his soul burns in Hell!"

With a sense of regret, Detective Hill decided there was no sense in questioning her further. Instead he decided to go investigate the scene of the stolen automobile.

"I'm sincerely sorry for your loss, Miss Redman," he offered.

She starred at him blankly.

Cutting his losses, he exited the house.

* * *

An hour earlier, Domonic "Crowbar" Coroza had stolen a 1964 greyish-blue Pontiac Bonneville. He had been paid five thousand dollars to break a guy's legs. The 'hit' lived in a small community adjacent to Blossom Hills called Sharonville, on Sharonville Drive. Crowbar parked the stolen Bonneville at the corner, then waited alongside Jeff Miles' house with a baseball bat. As Jeff exited his house, and before he reached his car, Crowbar stepped out of the shadows and swung the bat aiming for his knee caps. Jeff screamed in agonizing pain and covered his knees with both hands. For good measure, Crowbar gave him a parting blow to the head. Then he raced to the stolen car, keyed the ignition, and pressed the gas pedal down hard tearing up grass and spewing gravel. The tires squealed as they hit dry pavement. Crowbar made several quick turns and the car went airborne as it went over a hill on Dupont Avenue. He never saw the little girl, not that it would have made any difference. The only thing important to Crowbar was that he made good his escape.

* * *

A long week had gone by with no further information coming in on the hit and run of Charlotte Redman. Feeling none to good concerning the lack of results, Detective Hill decided to pay his respects to the grieving mother by attending the funeral. There was no viewing for Charlotte Lynn Redman. She was buried in a closed casket. Sergeant Hill stood across from Nicole, on the opposite side of the casket. He starred looking at the auburn haired, attractive, but sad looking woman, wondering how she was managing to hold up under the pressure of her grief. Family, friends, and neighbors crowded the gravesite. The sky was overcast, and colorful leaves fell from the trees, slowly making their way to the ground.

Nicole stood motionless, a single tear running down her face.

After the services were over, Sergeant Hill walked over to offer his condolences, and whispered. "I'm so sorry for your loss. I promise that I will find the person responsible for this."

"Person? Don't you mean monster?" Nicole looked around at the departing mourners, then coldly said. "All of you bastards are alike. Her own father didn't even make arrangements to come for the funeral."

Understanding that her anger was motivated by grief, Hill offered. "The car was reported stolen from the Harrendale Mall in Glen Burnie. We believe that it was used as the getaway car in an assault that took place on Sharonville Drive minutes before the accident."

"Accident?" Nicole shouted, drawing the attention of others. "Is that what you are calling it? An Accident? My baby was murdered! And, that murderer just kept on going."

Sergeant Hill sighed his regret. "You're right, but at the moment I don't know what else to say."

"Me neither, Detective." Nicole gave him a long look, then turned to walk away.

* * *

"Mutha fucker!" Harold Bennett screamed, "I just wanted the guy's legs broke. I didn't want him killed. What part of that didn't you understand?"

"He's not dead," Tony Bedsoe calmly replied. Tony had acted as the middle man. Jeff Miles was boning Harold Bennett's wife, and Harold wanted to put him out of commission for a while, that's all.

"He's not dead yet, but he's in the hospital wrapped up like a mummy with more tubes in his ass than either of us can count. He's in critical condition, on life support, and in a coma. If he does live, the doctors think he will, more than likely, be comatose. He's a friggin' vegetable! And, if he doesn't live, that's murder. Are you going to make me an accomplice to murder?"

"Of course not." Tony snapped, regretting his having gotten involved.

Tony was the bouncer/doorman and manager of the Blue Onion on Howard Street. He was in his late twenties, short, stocky, and with light brown hair. There was nothing outstanding about him other than his noticeably broken nose. It was pushed far to the right. He always wore turtleneck sweaters, even in the summer. Tony had an annoying habit of playing with a quarter. At first, he kept his right hand in his pants pocket and rolled one quarter over another – again…and again. When someone taught him how to roll a quarter through his fingers, one at a time, he added flipping the coin in the air and catching it with the same hand. The quarter stayed in constant motion, and Tony never tired of playing the game. But, for the most part, Tony was a nobody. He met Domonic when they both worked construction. He knew Dominic was a 'hitman', and when the opportunity came for him to set something up, it gave Tony a sense of importance. He could finally be the man.

The Blue Onion was a small Club. The bar was lined with stools and there were about six booths lining a wall. Three, sometimes four dancers worked the floor hustling drunken sailors and local chumps. The girls were required to dance on top of the bar for fifteen minutes. When one came down, another went up. A glass of champagne cost eight bucks. If a patron bought a bottle it cost one hundred dollars, but he shared a booth until the bottle was empty. That's how the girls made their money. They were paid commission, two dollars and fifty cents for every glass of champagne and twenty-five dollars for a bottle. The seasoned, or more experienced girls, carried an empty bottle of Seven-up with them, and spit the champagne into the empty bottle.

"I need the money that you owe," Tony was telling Harold.

"Let's wait and see what happens to Jeff Miles," Harold countered, knowing that Jeff was still on life support.

"No, I need the money now." Tony snapped, angrily.

"That's not going to happen. If Jeff dies I'm not paying shit."

"You're making a big mistake. I'm telling you, you're fucking with the wrong people."

Harold stood six two, weighed two hundred and fifty pounds, and use to be a boxer in his youth, twice winning golden glove titles. In his older years the beer had hit its mark and love handles hung slightly over his belt. All of his life he had worked with his hands, the last ten spent laboring away at Bethlehem Steel. It was a hot, demanding job, but Harold had a family of five to support. He married his childhood sweetheart and thought they were living a fairytale existence, pretty much the American dream. That was, until his best friend told him that his wife was having an affair with Jeff Miles.

CHAPTER TWO
THE FLOATER

Leroy was seven years old. After school, he and his pal, Ronnie, decided to go crabbing. So, they grabbed their nets and headed for the Chesapeake Bay. Ronnie's nickname was 'Twinkie'. He was a year older and much heavier than Leroy. He was given the nickname 'Twinkie' because of his appetite for Hostess Twinkies. In less than two minutes, Ronnie could devour an entire box of Twinkies. A local merchant paid the boys twenty-five cents for every crab they brought him. Today was a good day. So far, they had managed to catch four crabs. Hoping to relocate to a better area, they approached a weeded area they had successfully crabbed in the past. As they neared the weeded area, a foul stench fell over them. It was unlike anything they had ever smelled before.

"What's that?" Leroy asked, sniffing the air.

"I don't know." Ronnie frowned.

Then they saw it, two legs floating in the water. Crabs frantically scattered at their approach.

Leroy and Twinkie stopped dead in their tracks, turned to look at each other, then ran away just as fast as their little feet could carry them. Reaching Leroy's house a half a block away, breathlessly they entered the kitchen through the back door. Leroy snatched up the phone and called the police.

"Please state your emergency!"

"There's a body in Chesapeake Bay, and the crabs are eating it." Leroy screamed.

"Is your mother or father at home?"

"No! But, hurry up. Come quick. The crabs are eating it." Leroy screamed a second time.

"Please, calm down. Are you sure it's a body?"

"Yes!"

"Is it a man or woman?"

"I don't know."

"Is it an adult or child?"

"It's a white body. It stinks! And the crabs are eating it."

Thirty minutes later the police pulled the body from the water. Detectives from the Baltimore City Homicide Division were present, asking questions and taking notes. The crabs had feasted on the corpse, the face having been eaten away to the bone. The body was determined to be a Caucasian female, twenty to thirty years of age. It was assumed that she died from the multiple stab wounds they discovered to her chest.

An official autopsy would later confirm how right they were. Due to the body being submerged in water, and the advanced decomposition and bloating, it would be hard to determine the exact time of death. Still, the Coroner was willing to estimate the time of death to be about seventy-two hours ago.

"Do you have any witnesses." Detective Marks asked the Harbor Master.

"Right over there." He pointed to the two young black boys.

"Oh. That's just fantastic." Detective Marks growled, shaking his head from side to side. He gingerly walked over to the boys, then asked. "Did either of you see anything out of the ordinary."

"Crabs." Leroy snapped. "There were a lot of crabs eating the body."

Twinkie shrugged his shoulders, then added. "I never knew dead people stank so bad."

"Thanks a lot." Marks replied sarcastically. He knew that until the body was identified, the investigation was a dead end.

* * *

The Baltimore Sun's Headlines read 'MURDER IN THE HARBOR', and reported the identity of the female victim as being a Jane Doe. An unidentifiable victim.

A smaller article reported on a assault that took place in Sharon-ville, identifying the brutally beaten victim by the name of Jeff Miles. Reading the account of the incident, Nicole was reminded of the information given to her by Detective Hill concerning the stolen car being linked to the assault. Jeff Miles was at the Trauma Care Unit at Maryland University Hospital, where he was listed in critical condition.

Nicole was livid. There was no mention of her daughter's murder. It was at that moment she decided to take matters into her own hands. If the police were not going to find Charlotte's killer, then as a mother she would. She would start by paying Jeff Miles a visit in the hospital.

Half an hour later, she approached the front reception desk at the Hospital.

"May I help you," the woman behind the counter asked.

"Yes. Do you have a patient registered as a, Mr. Jeff Miles?"

The receptionist checked, then reported. "Yes, we do. Mr. Miles is in room 602."

"Thank you." Nicole replied, then walked to the nearest elevator. The door chimed and opened. She stepped inside, pressing the button for the sixth floor. When the elevator stopped, she took a deep breath. The door opened, and she stepped out.

"Where are you going darling," a friendly nurse asked.

"Room 602."

"Down the hall, last room on your left." The nurse smiled, then continued down the tiled hallway, pushing a cart loaded with medicine.

Nicole stood outside the door listening for voices, or movement. She heard nothing, so she stepped inside the room and looked around. There were two hospital beds, but one of them was empty. At the foot of the occupied bed there was a medical chart in a wire basket. Both of Jeff's legs were in casts and hanging from slings. His head was wrapped in bandages and he lay motionless on the bed. Nicole sat down in a chair next to him, and in sympathy took his hand. Although they were complete strangers, she felt a deep connection to this man and a great sorrow for his wife.

"What are you doing here, Miss Redman," she heard a voice behind her ask. She looked up. Detective Hill stood framed in the doorway.

"What are you doing here," she asked him.

"I come here every night, hoping he's awake. I guess I'm just hoping to get a break."

"I saw his name in the newspaper." Nicole said quietly.

"You need to leave this in my hands and go home."

"Has his wife given you information?"

"Nothing that is of any help."

"Maybe she would feel more comfortable talking to me?" Nicole offered.

"No," he replied flatly.

"Did you see the newspaper? They haven't reported anything about Charlotte's murder," she burst into tears.

Sergeant Hill hesitated for a brief second before moving to put his arms around her in an effort to comfort her. He whispered. "You should go home, Miss Redman. Newspapers don't report on hit and run accidents. I promise that I will call you as soon as I have something."

"Accident?" Nicole snapped. "It's not an accident!"

"I'm on your side," Hill pointed out.

"Thank you," she replied. He cared and Nicole felt it.

* * *

"Tony, I don't know how much clearer I can make this. I want my money! I don't give a fuck if you have to sell your old lady's ass. Or yours. I don't care if you have to suck two thousand five hundred dicks. If you don't have my money Friday night, there's going to be nothing left to talk about. Do we understand each other?"

"Domonic, give me a break here. I did a guy a favor. He's pissed. You're pissed."

"He has no reason to be pissed. I busted the guy up real good."

"Too good! The guy only wanted the guys leg broke to put him out of commission because he was boning his old lady. The guy's in a friggin' coma. He may be comatose, a vegetable. Or he may die. If he dies, that's murder. And my friend, he don't want to be no accomplice to murder."

"You tell your friend that if he ain't got my money by Friday that I'm going to break your right leg. If I don't have my money by Monday, I'm going to break your other leg. Then I'm going to start cutting off fingers, one by one, until you tell me who your friend is. If you run out of fingers, I'll take your shoes off. You will beg me to kill you! And when I'm finished with you, I'll be to see him. You tell your friend that for me." Domonic said all this with a smirk, then patted Tony on the cheek.

A few minutes after Domonic left the Blue Onion, Tony placed a call to Harold.

"Hello?"

"Harold?"

"I told you not to call my house."

"I've got to see you, now. It's urgent!"

"I'll be there in an hour."

"Okay. I'll see you then."

When Harold walked through the door twenty minutes later, Tony was on him. "I gotta have the money by Friday at the latest," he pleaded. Then he went on to tell Harold, word for word, what Domonic said. From Harold there was no emotion, fear, sympathy or understanding.

"Look," Harold snapped. "If there's an investigation, don't you think the police will check my phone to see who I'm calling and whose calling me. This isn't your first rodeo, use your friggin' head. If you have to call me, use a pay phone and don't use your real name.

Now, I don't know this character that you're dealing with, but he's not getting one dime if that guy dies. Not a dime!"

"I have a suggestion. Give me the money to pay him off, and if the guy dies I will make sure that you get the money back."

"That's not going to happen." Harold said flatly.

"I don't think you understand. This guy don't play no games. If I don't have his money, he's going to take it out on me!"

"Fuck that asshole."

"You fuck him." Tony said angrily, suddenly becoming very afraid for what might happen to him.

Harold just stared at him. Having nothing else to say, he calmly walked out.

CHAPTER THREE
THE WEE HOURS

At midnight, Gus pulled up in front of The Wee Hours in his fire engine red 1965 Chevrolet Supersport convertible. While he parked the car, he thought about how he had special ordered the car three years earlier, equipped with a 396 cubic inch, 325 horsepower engine, a 4-speed transmission, and factory air. In the same year he leased the building on Fleet street and built The Wee Hours. At the end of the street was Broadway, the harbor and docks only a few blocks away. Fleet street being one of the few areas left in Baltimore paved in red brick. The street lighting was poor, but when the Club was open for business, the yellow porch light, located high on the front of the building, made it visible from a block away.

Exiting the car and locking it, Gus went to unlock the black steel mesh security door of the Club. He pushed and secured it to the side of the building before opening the inner door to the after-hour club.

Flipping a light switch just inside the entrance, he closed the door behind him.

Having worked construction for the better part of his life, Gus used his experience to finish the outside of the building with yellow vinyl siding, while a cubby-hole at the entrance protected patrons from the harsh elements. The customers greatly appreciated the shelter, especially during the winter months. Inside, the walls were covered in pine paneling. Yellow recessed lights were spaced six feet apart around the room. The floor was covered in red indoor/outdoor carpet. The inside was fairly small, perhaps twenty feet wide by thirty-five feet in length. It was large enough to accommodate five tables on each wall and five tables with four chairs in the center of the room. There was also a small stage with a jukebox next to it. At the rear of the room there was an eight foot long, four feet high, counter with a cash register sitting on top of it to the far left. By law, after-hour clubs were only permitted to sell nonalcoholic beverages which was served in clear plastic cups filled with ice. Seven-Up and Coca-Cola were favored. Beyond the bar was a short hallway with doors leading to other parts of the building. The first door on the right was made of heavy steel, and a stairway led to the upstairs were there were four rooms. One was used for poker games. Gus used one for a bedroom, another for a bathroom, and the last for storage. Continuing down the paneled hallway, the second door on the right opened to Gus' private office. As long as the office door was kept locked during business hours, it was legal for liquor to be kept inside. The last door on the right was the public rest-room, to be used by either gender. For the sake of privacy, the door was kept locked. If a customer needed to use the rest-room, Rose, who tended the bar and answered the phone would let them in. At the end of the hallway there was a large kitchen equipped with a white refrigerator, a double stainless steel sink, and a dart board. The dart board was Gus' hustle, and there were a lot of wagers placed on dart games.

The Wee Hours was a "Members Only" club with a cover charge of two dollars. That was Gus' way of keeping out the riff raff and less desirables. It was "Members Only" if Gus did not approve of a customer's looks, dress, or mannerism. The rules were simple. There were no drugs allowed in the club and patrons were not permitted to bring liquor into the after-hour club. If a prostitute took 'a trick' out of the club, she paid Gus fifteen dollars. Well-known customers could purchase shots of whiskey, rum, or vodka, for four dollars. It was Rose's responsibility to go into Gus' private office and make the drinks. In the event of a raid, everyone was informed to pour the drinks on the floor. For this reason, Gus had the carpet cleaned monthly.

By three o'clock in the morning, the club reached full capacity and people were turned away at the door unless they were there to gamble.up. Or, unless you were Domonic Coroza. No one dared refuse Domonic entrance to the club. At the Wee Hours. Domonic had his own table, placed in a far corner next to the bar, providing him with an unobstructed view of the room with his back to the wall. Over the years Domonic had made many enemies and very few friends. He demanded respect with his utter ruthlessness, knowing that in his world it was never freely given. Due to the presence of a new door-man, on this night Domonic was not given immediate entrance.

Gus, and three other players were in the back shooting darts for a hundred dollars a game when the new doorman, Alex, entered the room. He approached to whisper in Gus' ear." There's a guy at the door waiting to get in. He told me to tell you that his name is Domonic Coroza."

"Shit!" Gus cursed. "Apologize for keeping him waiting. Don't charge him a cover charge. Just let him in."

Gus rushed to Domonic's favored table, apologized to the couple sitting there, and told them they had to move. On every table there was a red glass bowl wrapped in fishnet with a scented candle inside; making for a nice atmosphere. Gus asked Rose for a fresh candle, lit it, and wiped the table clean. At that moment Domonic came striding around the other club members towards the table, a frown darkening his brow.

"How are you doing, Crowbar?" Gus greeted him, offering his hand in friendship. Only those closest to Domonic dared to call him by his nickname.

"Good," he replied, ignoring Gus's outstretched hand. Gus let his hand drop to his side.

Crowbar frowned. "You need to do something about the parking. I had to park my Coupe Deville on the opposite side of the street."

Noticing the band-aid on Domonic's face, Gus asked. "What hap-pened?"

"What the hell you concerned with a cut on my face for. I cut my-self shaving this morning."

Gus immediately knew it to be a lie. In hindsight, it was a foolish question for him to ask. "Gotta be more careful" Gus smiled, then motioned for Rose to give Domonic a drink. "Whatever he wants. On the house."

"How's business been," Crowbar asked.

"Just fair." Gus answered, not really wanting him to know his business." Now, if you will excuse me, I have a dart game in progress and I'm holding my pigeons up. If you need anything, just holler."

Domonic chuckled at Gus' referring to his opponents as 'Pigeons'. He picked the lighted candle up and blew it out, preferring to sit in the darkness. It was half an hour later when the club's phone rang. "It's for you, Gus." Rose yelled.

"Hello?" Gus snatched up the receiver sounding ticked off. He was on a roll and up several hundred dollars shooting darts, and did not want anything to disturb his groove.

"Did you read the newspaper this morning?" Jerry Everhart, a local pimp asked.

"Yeah, I did. But could you be more specific?"

"Did you read about the unidentified female corpse found floating in the harbor?"

"I saw it." Gus replied.

"I think that was my girl, Missy. The description fits her and she's missing."

"Have the police made a positive identification?"

"Not that I'm aware of. I'm not about to run down to the police station and volunteer that she's one of my whores."

"I can't say that I blame you." Gus laughed at the thought.

"Missy was a good girl and she was a money making bitch. I swear, if the girl in the harbor is Missy and I find out who killed her, I will personally cut the son of a bitch's nuts off."

"Let's hope it's not her."

"Well, if it's not her I'm going to kill the friggin' bitch for running out on me!"

* * *

Friday afternoon, Domonic called Tony at the Blue Onion and

asked for his money.

"The cock sucker wouldn't give me the money. He said fuck me, and fuck you. He said he ain't paying another dime until he finds out if the guy's gonna live."

"Is that what he said?"

"Yeah, Domonic. I swear I'm giving it to you straight."

"I'll talk to you later."

"I hope you're not upset with me. I tried to collect the friggin' money." Tony protested, but he was already speaking into the wind. Domonic had hung up.

Around midnight a girl ran into the Blue Onion, "Help! Please somebody help! He's killing my girlfriend," she screamed, tears pouring from her eyes.

Tony was bellied up to the bar, rolling a quarter through his fingers. Without hesitation, he hurriedly followed the woman out of the front door, completely unaware that he was the only customer to do so. He had just enough time to note the woman take off running down the street.

"Smack!"

"Ahhh!" His scream broke the silence of the night as he fell to the ground in agonizing pain, his left leg on fire with pain.

Domonic stood over him holding a Louisville slugger baseball bat. "What did I tell you, you blood sucker?"

Tony tried desperately to crawl away from him while protecting his head. "Oh, my God," he moaned.

"Didn't I tell you that if you didn't have my money I was going to break your right leg?" Domonic growled. "Didn't I tell you that," he repeated.

"You told me," Tony cried.

"Well, that's your left leg. I believe I said I was going to start with your right one." Domonic reflected in a casual way, then raised the bat for a second swing.

"No! No! Please don't, Domonic." Tony pleaded, getting Domenic to halt his swing.

Domonic glanced briefly around to make sure the street was still deserted. He then leaned down over the prone man. "Do you know what's going to happen Monday if you don't have my money?"

Tony coward away. "Yes!"

"I sure hope we don't have to have this conversation again."

"We won't," Tony swore.

* * *

Tony called Harold from the hospital, explaining that he needed to talk to him right away. Making it clear that it was urgent.

"I told you not to call my house." Harold whispered.

"I'm at the Baltimore Memorial Hospital. I'm in the emergency room. Come pick me up right now."

Exactly forty-three minutes later Harold walked into the lobby. By which time Tony was sitting in a chair sporting a white cast that extended from his ankle to his hip, crutches resting against a vacant chair to his right. Tony stood, put a crutch under each arm and said. "I told you. I told you the guy's a friggin' maniac. Now, help me out to your car."

Harold opened the passenger door, pushed the seat back and Tony squeezed in. As Harold sat down in the driver's seat, he found himself looking down the barrel of Tony's Colt.45.

"You son of a bitch! I did you a favor. You're going to give me the friggin' money. I told you that mutha fucker don't play no games. I told you!"

"You do understand why I'm holding it up," Harold asked.

"Fuck you! Your wife don't know you know she's been fucking some other guy. Did you tell anyone else?"

"Of course not!"

"Then besides the hired hitman, there's only two people who know. Me and you. He's not gonna talk. I'm not gonna talk. So how can anything be linked back to you?"

"Alright. I'll give you the money." Reluctantly, Harold drove to the bank, withdrew twenty-five hundred dollars and gave it to Tony.

* * *

Detective Marks was in his office at the Baltimore City Police Department looking over the coroner and toxicology reports regarding his Jane Doe corpse. There were five stab wounds. Two to the upper torso and three to the stomach. Needle marks were found on both arms, indicating that the victim was a junkie, and a large quantity of heroin found in her system confirmed that. The coroners report noted one small scar on her right knee and a star tattooed on her right shoulder. Blood and semen were found in her anal canal. Two broken fingernails indicated a struggle with her attacker, Marks called over a senior detective.

"What does this mean?" Detective Marks asked, pointing to a written comment.

"Someone busted her rear cherry," the senior detective retorted, shaking his head in disgust.

"Well, she obviously didn't like it." Detective Marks replied, pointing out the two broken fingernails in the report.

* * *

Meanwhile, at the Anne Arundel County Sheriff's Department, Sergeant Hill received the monthly phone statement from AT&T of Jeff Miles' residence. In one month, twenty calls were placed to Harold and Marsha Bennett's home phone, all before Two O'Clock in the afternoon. With a little police work, Detective Hill discovered that Harold Bennett worked five days a week at Bethlehem Steel in Sparrows Point, which meant the calls couldn't possibly have been made to Harold. He requested that AT&T provide him with a copy of the monthly billing for the Bennett residence. Next, he placed a call to the Bennett residence.

"Hello." A soft spoken woman answered.

"Mrs. Bennett?"

"Speaking."

"Mrs. Bennett, this is Detective Hill from the Anne Arundel County Sheriff's Department. I am investigating an assault on a Jeff Miles and your name has come up, but you are not a suspect. Would it be possible for you to come down to the station and speak with me? I would like to spare you any embarrassment."

"Of course, I'll be right down."

Twenty minutes later, Marsha Bennett parked her white Mustang convertible in the parking lot of the Sheriff's Department and walked through the front entrance.

Sergeant Hill looked out the window of his second floor office and saw her walking down the sidewalk. He walked downstairs, introduced himself, and escorted her upstairs. They sat at his desk, across from one another.

"Can I get you a cup of coffee," he offered.

"No thank you," she politely declined.

"Mrs. Bennett…"

"Please call me, Marsha," she smiled, crossing one long bare leg over the other. Her eyes were brown, her teeth like pearls, and she had the most beautiful complexion of any woman he had ever met.

"Do you know a Jeff Miles?"

"No, I don't," she lied.

"Do you have any idea why there's twenty calls to your home last month, all before Two O'Clock in the afternoon, and from Jeff Miles residence?"

"I don't know." Marsha squirmed.

"Mrs. Bennett, there are a number of other phone numbers subject to scrutiny. Two from massage parlors. I am trying to spare you any unnecessary embarrassment, but I hope you understand that I have to do my job."

"I have nothing further to say. Am I under arrest for something?"

"No. You are free to go. But would you please tell your husband that I will be calling to set-up an appointment with him."

"My husband has nothing to do with this! What exactly is it that you're investigating?"

"Jeff Miles is in the hospital. One morning he woke up, stepped outside his house and as he walked to his car to go to work, he was assaulted with a baseball bat. He is in the hospital, in critical condition, and in a coma. He may not survive. The man who assaulted him escaped in a stolen car. In fleeing the scene, he ran over a six year old little girl who was playing hopscotch in front of her house. I don't believe you have any involvement in this. But the investigation has led me to you and I need answers."

"Jeff Miles was a client. He wouldn't harm a fly. I have no idea why anyone would want to harm him."

"A client?"

"I am a working girl. My husband knows nothing about that. Harold is a good man, and he works hard to support his family."

"At this point, I have no reason to tell him. Thank you for your cooperation." Detective Hill replied.

"Thank you!"

"I still may need to speak to your husband."

"I understand." Marsha replied, hoping it would never happen.

"If I do need to speak to him, I won't mention that you're a working girl unless it's absolutely necessary." Detective Hill added.

Marsha smiled. Then as a second thought asked. "What happened to the little girl?"

"She died instantly." Hill told her solemnly.

"Oh, my God! That's so sad," she sighed, thinking to herself that it could have just as easily been one of her children.

CHAPTER FOUR
THE INVESTIGATIONS

There were no links between the body found in the Bay and the beating of Jeff Miles. The two investigators had never met, but the one thing they shared in common was frustration. Detective Marks spent days trying to hunt down and discover possible witnesses in the stabbing death of the Harbor Bay woman. So far everyone he spoke to led him to one dead end after another, leading to nothing left to follow-up on. Sergeant Hill's luck was no better, but he was more hopeful. He had a possible link between the assault on Jeff Miles and the death of Charlotte Lynn Redman. A neighbor clearly was able to place a blue Buick or Pontiac parked in the grass on Sharonville Drive, which was very near the location where Miles had been beaten. He was certain the description of the car directly linked it to the Bonneville and the hit and run of Charlotte. However, if Jeff Miles did not regain consciousness, the case was more than likely at a dead end.

There were no eyewitnesses and no fingerprints. Sergeant Hill had made a promise to himself and he would not rest until he exhausted every possible lead. There were still two people he wanted to interview, Jeff's wife Vivian and Harold Bennett. He was able to speak briefly to Vivian the morning of the attack, but she was badly shaken and Sergeant Hill was a compassionate man. At the time he did not feel it appropriate to question her in great detail. He also wanted to return to the scene where the attack took place. There was always the remote possibility of something having been overlooked, some stone unturned. He reasoned that the longer an investigation lasted, time became an investigator's worst enemy.

Sergeant Hill looked at his watch, then picked up the phone to dial Nicole's number. It was eight o' clock in the morning.

While waiting for the phone to be answered, he poured himself a cup of coffee, adding creamer and two lumps of sugar. As he stirred the coffee, the phone continued to ring. After the twelfth ring, he hung up, wondering where she could be. He dialed the number for Vivian Miles. On the third ring, she answered. "Hello?"

"Good morning, Mrs. Miles. This is Sergeant Hill from the Anne Arundel County Sheriff's Department. I just missed you at the hospital last night. When I arrived, the nurse said you had just left. Are you going to be home this morning? I would like to take a second look around the house and have a talk with you. That's if you're available."

"I have an appointment at the hospital at Two O'Clock this afternoon. My husband's physicians have requested a consultation. I'm not exactly sure what that means."

"How about if I come over in about forty-five minutes?"

"That would be fine."

Forty minutes later, Sergeant Hill parked his dark blue Ford Maverick at the curb in front of the residence of Vivian and Jeff Miles. It was a two story home with white vinyl siding and black shutters. There were shrubs planted along the front of the house, with a circular garden dead center in the front yard, and in the middle of this garden stood a long flag pole. An American flag topped the pole and waved slowly in the wind. There was a cement double car driveway off to the right of the house, while a long cemented walkway led up to the front door. The house itself was a standard three bedroom, one and a half bath with finished basement, the builder having modeled all of the homes in Sharonville from pretty much the same floor plan. Jeff's blood was still imminent on the driveway, and that was troublesome for even a seasoned investigator such as himself. Why had no one offered or taken the time out to clean up the blood spill? He knew every time Vivian stepped outside it must be a constant reminder.

He walked to the front door and rang the doorbell. Within seconds Vivian opened the door, smiled and said. "Hi."

"Do you have any bleach," he asked.

"Yes, of course. Why?"

"May I use it? And would you please open the garage door," Vivian did as he asked without questioning him further.

Inside the garage Sergeant Hill found a thick bristle push broom with a long wooden handle, and a garden hose rolled into a coil hanging neatly from a hook next to a work bench. Vivian walked out of the house while he was connecting the garden hose to an outside faucet. He looked up. She was still wearing a white dressing gown and pink fluffy house slippers. Her hair was still in curlers, but she thoughtfully hid those beneath a scarf. She wore no makeup on her face and her smile was genuine.

"This is all I have," she reported, holding out a gallon jug of Clorox bleach in her right hand.

Sergeant Hill felt the contents of the jug. It was still half full. "It's plenty," he replied, spraying water on the blood stained driveway.

"You don 't have to do that," she said, trying to be polite.

"I know." Hill smiled. "But if it bothers me, I'm sure it bothers you."

"Yes, it does." Vivian admitted. "I appreciate your concern!"

"Protect and serve. It's an officer's duty," he smiled. Sergeant Hill twice scrubbed the blood spill with bleach, not all of the blood coming up; when he finished the blot slowly blended in with the other stains of the driveway. He rolled up the garden hose and returned it to the hook in the garage, then returned the broom to its rightful place. Jeff Miles seemed to be a man that kept a very neat garage, everything in its own special place. Even the lawn-mower looked polished. When he was finished, he walked to the side of the house, visualized where he thought the attacker may have stood, and tried to guess in which direction he ran to make good his escape.

"Can I offer you a cup of coffee?" Vivian asked, more curious as to what he was doing, but not wanting to ask.

"Yes. Thank you."

"How would you like it?"

"Do you have creamer?"

"No, but I have milk."

"Milk and two sugars will be fine."

They walked inside the house together and sat down at the kitchen table. Hill noticed the house was meticulously maintained. There were ducks everywhere.

"I see you like ducks," he chuckled.

There was a duck cookie jar on the kitchen counter. Duck salt and pepper shakers sitting on the kitchen table. A duck clock. White canisters on the kitchen counter with painted ducks, and there were ducks on the curtains above the kitchen sink.

"Don't you make fun of my ducks," she giggled like a little girl.

Sergeant Hill laughed. Then waited until she served him a cup of piping hot coffee before asking. "Do you have any idea who may have wanted to harm your husband."

"No."

"Did he have any enemies that you're aware of?"

"No. Everyone simply adored Jeff."

"One of your neighbors called and reported a blue car parked in the grass at the corner when she left to go to the grocery store. When she returned a short time later the car was gone. There was a stolen dark blue Pontiac Bonneville found abandoned at the I.G.A. grocery store on Fort Smallwood Road. It was stolen an hour before the assault. It's been identified as the vehicle that ran over a six year old girl playing hopscotch in the street. She was killed instantly."

"My daughter Tara is six years old. She hasn't said much, but she knew the little girl that was killed. Her name is Charlotte. They were classmates. We had no idea there was a possible connection. It's so terrible. I hope you catch the animal responsible!"

"Your husband is a steel worker?"

"Yes. Jeff served eight years in the Marines. He was in Special Forces. Five years ago we moved here and he went to work for Bethlehem Steel. It took him five years to get to the day shift. He was scheduled to start working the day shift the day after he was assaulted."

"Has his condition improved any?"

"No. Well, not that I'm aware of. I'm not sure what prognosis his physician will render this afternoon. We have two children. My son Todd is ten. Yesterday he came home from school with a black eye. One of the other kids laughed and teased that his daddy was a fruit. He meant vegetable, I'm sure. My guess is he overheard his parents talking about the attack and Jeff's condition. Todd hit the kid for talking about his father, and the bully blackened his eye. The school called and I had to pick up my son. I'm not sure what I'm supposed to say or do. My kids love their father. Jeff is a very good father and husband."

"I wish I knew what to tell you to do. But, I don't. I'm not married, and have no children. It's just a sad state of affairs."

"Yes, it is." Vivian agreed, then offered. "Would you care for another cup of coffee?"

"No, thank you. I've got to get going."

* * *

Sergeant Hill drove to Nicole's house. It was only a half mile away in the neighboring community of Blossom Hills. He parked in the driveway, walked to the front door and knocked. No one answered, so he peered through the open curtains at the right of the door, and into the living-room. There was no movement and he could see straight through into the kitchen.

"Ain't nobody been there since the little girl got killed." An elderly lady shouted from across the street.

"Any idea where she might have gone?"

"Nope. She pretty much kept to herself."

"If you should see her, would you ask her to call Sergeant Hill?"

"You got a card?"

Sergeant Hill walked across the street and handed the elderly neighbor one of his cards.

"I'm not too good at remembering names, but if I see her I'll be sure to give her your card. I'll tell her that you stopped by and want her to call you."

"Thank you." Sergeant Hill smiled.

"You're most welcome." The old lady replied, offering a toothless grin.

* * *

"I don't want to hear it! You owe me, you rotten bastard. What kind of man doesn't attend his own daughter's funeral?"

"I told you I was out of town on a business trip." Charlie shouted back.

"Business trip? Is that what you call it? I'm thinking you were laying in the sun on a blanket on a beach in Miami, fucking your whores and buying drugs. Charlie, that's not a fuckin' business trip." Nicole opened an ounce of powder cocaine, made double lines two inches long and snorted a line into each nostril. She tilted her head backwards and sniffed hard several times.

"What do you want, Nicole?"

"What do I want? I want to know who murdered our daughter. I want to cut his balls off, and feed his ass to the sharks. That's what I want."

"I have no idea who's responsible. What is it you expect me to do?"

"I don't know, but it's driving me nuts!" Nicole screamed.

"Surely, you understand there's nothing either of us can do?"

"All I know is every waking moment I see that damn car coming over the hill and landing on top of Charlotte. I fall to my knees and scream in horror. Charlie, I have to find my baby's murderer. Do you know what the police call her death?" Nicole asked, looking in Charlie's eyes.

"What?"

"An accident! Charlotte's death is ruled a hit and run accident."

* * *

Sergeant Hill was in his office sitting at his desk, creating files, shuffling through papers and preparing a report about his interview with Vivian Miles. He wondered why Jeff had strayed? There was nothing in his background to support infidelity. Jeff was an ex-Marine, which was a testament to his character. He was a family man in every sense of the word. His kids loved him and Vivian was pleasing to the eyes. So why would Jeff seek the services of a Call Girl?

"Hey Sarge." A junior detective interrupted his thoughts. "The police report on the stolen Bonneville just came in." He handed over the report to Hill.

The report was brief. The vehicle belonged to a retired worker, his name was Gregory Koch. The report included his name, address, and phone number. Koch stated that he worked night security at the Harrendale Mall, in an effort to supplement his income. He parked the car when he arrived at work, and when he was ready to leave, it was gone. From Hill's point of view there was no reason to contact him, he would be worthless as a witness.

Detective Hill placed a call to Harold Bennett. Hopefully, he would be at home. Most steel workers did not work weekends, and it was Saturday. The phone rang several times before a female voice answered.

"Hello, Mrs. Bennett?"

"Yes."

"This is Detective Hill. Real quick. I have no reason to share information regarding your personal affairs with your husband, but I do need to speak to him."

"Thank you," she replied, then yelled. "Harold, it's for you!"

A few minutes later, Harold came on the line. "Hello, this is Harold Bennett. May I ask whose calling?"

"My name is Detective Sergeant Hill. I am with the Sheriff's Department for Anne Arundel County, and I need to speak to you regarding a case I've been assigned. I would prefer to do that sometime today. Either at the station, or I can meet you somewhere."

"May I ask what this is about?"

"I will explain when we meet."

"Where is the Sheriffs station located?"

"It's in Millersville." Detective Hill gave directions, and Harold said that he would be there within the hour.

"What was that about." Marsha asked her husband, playing dumb.

"I don't exactly know," Harold answered. For the first time in his life Harold was scared and trying hard to maintain his composure. He wondered how it was possible for his name to come up?

* * *

"Emergency services. Please state your emergency?"

"Tell Detective Marks at the Baltimore City Homicide Division that the dead girl found in the Harbor is Sheila Watts. Her nickname is Missy and she was a known prostitute."

"May I have your name and phone number, please?"

Click… the line went dead.

* * *

Harold Bennett parked his shiny black Ford Bronco in the parking lot of the Anne Arundel County Sheriff's Department. He walked into the building, stopped at the receptionist desk, and asked for Detective Sergeant Hill. Within minutes, Hill greeted Harold with a smile and a friendly handshake.

"Let's go upstairs where we can talk without any interruptions. Can I offer you a cup of coffee?"

"No thanks." Harold replied flatly. Sergeant Hill noticed that Harold was a good two inches taller than himself. His hands were calloused and his handshake had been firm. He supposed Harold would be a hard man to reckon with in a fight.

"Are you sure I can't get you a cup of coffee?"

"No thanks." Harold repeated.

"Mind if I have one?" Sergeant Hill asked.

"Help yourself, but I didn't come all the way down here for a coffee break. I would appreciate you not wasting my time and getting right to the point."

"Of course. Your name has come up in my investigation."

"Could you please be more specific?"

"Do you know a Jeff Miles?"

"No!"

"You both work at Bethlehem Steel."

"I don't know him." Harold repeated, his face blank and his eyes hard.

"Are you sure?" Hill pressed his doubt.

"I'm sure."

"A funny thing happened. One morning Jeff came out of his house to leave for work. As he's walking to his car, some guy steps out of the shadows swinging a baseball bat. He breaks both of Jeff's legs, then hits him in the head for good measure. Jeff's in the hospital in a coma, but that's not the worst part. As the guy was making good on his escape in a stolen vehicle, he runs down a six year old girl playing hopscotch in the middle of the street. She died in an instant. He just kept on going."

"It's a sad story and I wish I could help you. It wasn't me! I was at work and you're welcome to check. There is at least a hundred guys willing to vouch for my whereabouts. If you don't believe me check it out."

"Well, thanks for coming in." Hill nodded.

"By the way. You didn't say how it was that my name came up in your investigation."

"I'm sorry. I'm afraid that's privileged information."

"I get it. Have a nice day." Harold offered insincerely.

"You too!" Hill replied in the same tone.

* * *

"Detective Marks, I've got something for you." A junior Detective anxiously reported. "Someone called Emergency Services and reported the girl found in the Harbor is Sheila Watts. Her nickname is Missy, and she's a known prostitute."

"Did the caller identify themselves?"

"Nope. The caller hung up, but it was a female. I hope that helps."

"It certainly narrows the margins down to about a million." Detective Marks replied sarcastically.

CHAPTER FIVE
NO LIMITS

The office of the Baltimore City Homicide Division was crowded with detectives busy at work trying to track down leads to any open murder cases. Each detective was provided with a separate cubicle, lending a small amount of privacy to them in their search for the truth. At that moment, Detective Marks was pacing the floor at the front of one of the three conference rooms used for staff meetings. He was barking orders to four junior detectives.

"Okay, listen up! Someone called Emergency Services and put a name to our Jane Doe. Sheila 'Missy' Watts. W-A-T-T-S. Open up your phone directories, and hit the streets. Someone knows her! Somewhere out there she has a family. Our caller identified her as a known prostitute. Let's get some conformation on the identity, so we can make a positive identification. We run fingerprints. I want a full court press."

"Do we know the identity of the caller," a junior detective asked.

"No. But we do know the call was made from a pay phone on the North side of town and the caller was a female. That's all we have at this time."

* * *

Sergeant Hill returned to his office, sat down at his cluttered desk and checked for any incoming calls he might have missed. There was a brief message from the switchboard operator, informing him that Nicole Redman had called. She failed to leave a return phone number or message. Hill picked up the phone and dialed zero for the switchboard operator.

"How may I be of assistance," she answered.

"Hi, Nelly. Would you please call the Telephone Company and ask if they could trace the number Nicole Redman called from."

While waiting for Nelly to get back to him, Hill spent the next ten minutes trying to put the case together in his mind. He was certain that if he pushed hard enough he could link it all together. His phone rang.

"The number that call originated from is seven-three-five-two-three-seven-six," Nelly reported. Is there anything else I can help you with?"

"Not right now. Thanks Nelly." He hung up the phone and dialed the provided number. It rang six times before he heard a familiar voice on the other end.

"Hello?"

"Miss Redman."

"Sergeant Hill," she exclaimed, clearly surprised to hear his voice.

"I believe you called me earlier."

"I did, but you weren't in. How did you find out where I am?"

"I don't know where you are," he replied.

"Well, how did you get this number?"

"I have my sources," he chuckled.

"Aren't you the clever one?"

"How are you doing," he asked, his concern obvious. "I'm okay. Do you have anything new?"

"Would you like to get together sometime for a cup of coffee and talk? I'll give you an update."

"When?"

"Whenever it's convenient for you," he offered. "Where is a good place to meet?"

"That depends on where you are."

"I'm in Glen Burnie." Nicole thought about telling him exactly where she was, but decided not to. It was enough giving him the general location. She was certain he knew the area well.

"How about if we meet at the White Coffee Pot in the Harrendale Mall. Let's say in about forty-five minutes."

"I'll see you there."

Nicole hung up the phone and hurried into the bathroom. She quickly brushed her teeth and splashed some warm water on her face, using a clean towel to lightly pat her face dry. Running a brush through her hair and applying some lip gloss and eyeliner, she dressed in a pair of tight fitting Levi jeans and a white T-shirt. She seldom wore a bra. Then she slid her tiny feet into a pair of flip-flops, grabbed her car keys and ran out the door of Charlie's apartment. Charlie was sleeping, curled up in bed exhausted. She hated what she was doing to herself, but the drugs and sex seemed to help ease her pain. Regardless, the final results were all the same. When the party was over it brought her back to the cold reality that Charlotte was dead.

* * *

Nicole arrived at the White Coffee pot fifteen minutes before Detective Sergeant Hill. She parked, walked inside, picked a table in the rear of the restaurant and ordered coffee. She sat quietly watching the parking lot through a plate glass window. Sergeant Hill pulled in, parked his blue Ford Maverick beneath a light pole and walked inside. Surprisingly, the sight of him had her feeling good, and it never occurred to her to question why. It was enough to feel warm and bubbly like a school girl with her first crush.

"Hi Nicole," he smiled, taking the seat across from her.

When he spoke her name, it sent butterflies fluttering in the pit of her stomach. His walk, manners, charisma and contagious smile suddenly captured her heart.

"Hi yourself," she returned his smile, her eyes shinning in welcome. "I saw you drive up, so I ordered you a coffee. But I didn't know how you like it."

He was pleased to see her smile. It was beautiful. "One cream, two sugars."

"You like it sweet, huh? Is that how you like your women?"

"Naw. I like my women hot and sassy!"

Nicole laughed softly, looking into his eyes. "I promised I'd keep you updated."

Nicole was suddenly sober. "Yes, you did."

"Well, this is where I'm at. I called AT&T and obtained a copy of Jeff Miles' phone records. Incoming and outgoing for the last ninety days. There was more than thirty phone calls made from his house to the Bennett's residence last month. All before Two O'Clock. Harold Bennett works at Bethlehem Steel from 8 AM until 4 PM. Then, I called AT&T and obtained the monthly statement for the Bennett residence for the last ninety days.

"There were some questionable calls, several to the Bennett residence from known massage parlors. Armed with this information, I questioned Marsha, Harold Bennett's wife. At first she was reluctant to cooperate. I explained that I wasn't investigating her and I promised that I would try my best not to create any unnecessary problems for her. Admittedly, Marsha Bennett is a Call Girl and Jeff Miles was one of her customers. It was necessary for me to talk to Harold Bennett. At this point, he was the prime suspect. Harold was at work when the assault occurred. A hundred people have verified it. Oddly enough, both Harold Bennett and Jeff Miles worked at Bethlehem Steel, but Harold didn't know Jeff. He said Jeff worked nights and he worked days. Work records verify Jeff worked the night shift. So, I spoke with Jeff's wife, Vivian. There was nothing she could tell us. A neighbor did report she saw a blue Buick or Pontiac parked on the grass at the corner when she went to the store that morning. When she returned fifteen minutes later, the car was no longer there. That information at least gives us a possible connection. It's a lead to follow up on. I stopped by your house. The neighbor across the street stepped out of hers to tell me you hadn't been there since the accident. For some reason, I have not been able to get the picture of your neighbor out of my mind, and a fat lady in pink curlers isn't something that I care to remember."

"If you say accident one more time, I swear I'm going to hit you with something!"

"I'm sorry, Nicole. It's not my intent to diminish the cruel fate of your daughter. Honestly, I can't sleep at night for thinking about it."

"It's not an accident, it's murder! And I refuse to see it as anything else. And Marsha Bennett is a whore," she added angrily.

"I wouldn't call her that," Hill sighed.

"No? What would you call her? A prostitute, a Call girl, Lady of the night. Regardless of how you say it. It's all the same."

"Point well taken."

"What's your real name? And don't tell me Detective Hill."

"David Allen Hill. Would you like to know my family history?"

"Dave," she reflected. "I like it. Go ahead, give me the rest."

"I was born December 3, 1931 at John Hopkins Memorial Hospital in Baltimore, Maryland. I have two brothers and a younger sister. My father retired from the Baltimore County Sheriffs Department. My mother was a good wife, a loving mother and I miss her more every day. She passed away three years ago."

"I'm sorry!" Nicole replied, sincerely. Then she said. "You're thirty-seven. Have you ever been married?"

"Nope, and that's all you're getting from me."

"Where do we go from here?"

"I'm not sure. At this point there's always the possibility that the car that ran over Charlotte isn't even related to the assault. There are no concrete leads. I can't assume anything. For all we know your ex-husband didn't want to pay child support anymore. He could have paid someone…"

"Charlie?" Nicole interrupted, smiling. "You think he could be responsible?"

"He didn't attend her funeral, Nicole. I can't rule him out as a suspect."

"Do you know how stupid that sounds? In theory, he didn't want to pay child support, so he brought his daughter some chalk and told her to play hopscotch in the street on a specific day and time. Then he, or someone he hired, stole a car and ran her over." Nicole laughed again, placing her elbows on the table and the palms of her hands on her chin. Then she added. "Charlie was in Florida!"

"Is that what he told you?"

"Look. I know my husband. He's an asshole, but he had nothing to do with this. Besides, I bought the chalk."

"Regardless, I still have to interview him."

"Be my guest. But it's a waste of your time. Harold Bennett told you that he didn't know Jeff Miles. If that's true. How did he know Jeff Miles worked the night shift?"

Detective Hill pondered the thought. It was a good question. One he should have thought to ask. He left a tip on the table and went to pay the bill. While he was busy paying the cashier, Nicole joined him to help herself to a complimentary mint from the canister on the counter.

He walked Nicole to her car. As she unlocked the door to the Bug, he said. "I bet you're a good swimmer."

"I am. How did you know? I was the best swimmer on my high school swim team."

Sergeant Hill looked down at her polished toes in the flip-flops, laughed, and said. "Because you have duck feet."

"You don't like my feet," she smiled up at him with a flirtatious wink.

"They are very cute."

"See you, Detective Hill," she smiled, while climbing into her car. She started the Beetle and puttered away.

"Damnit," he cursed, wondering why he not thought to ask where she was staying.

The day was half over, but it was still gorgeous. The sun was shining. The sky was baby blue and filled with white clouds, looking like powder puffs in the gentle breeze. It was the lonely nights that he dreaded. At best, he would watch a football game and drink a six pack of beer with his feet propped up on the coffee table at his apartment.

It wasn't much to look forward to, but it filled an otherwise void in his life.

* * *

Shortly after midnight, Harold Bennett walked through the door of the Blue Onion on Howard street. It was an extremely hot night and Tony had left the front door propped open, hoping to let a little air into the humid room. There was not an empty stool in the bar. The music was loud and a girl in a g-string was shaking her tits and wiggling her ass, while dancing on the counter of the bar.

"Take it all off, baby!" A drunken sailor shouted. "Shake that thing!" Another patron yelled.

"Eat me!" The dancer yelled back.

It reminded Tony of a frenzy of hungry sharks at feeding time. Some fish took the bait, swallowing it hook, line, and sinker. At the end of the night most of the suckers would leave the bar with a hard on, and not a penny left in their pockets. Come the next payday they would return to repeat the same thing. Tony reasoned that it gave credence to the old adage 'a fool and his money shall soon part'. He looked as Harold joined him at the bar.

"How are you doing, Harold? How's the wife?" Tony asked.

"I need to talk to you in private. Now!"

"Sure, sure. Let's go to the office." Tony stood, balancing himself as he reached for his crutches. "Two more weeks and I get this friggin' cast off. I have to scratch and itch my leg with a friggin' coat hanger. Can you believe it?" Tony complained as they made their way to an office located at the rear of the bar.

Tony unlocked the door to the office. When the door swung open, Harold shoved Tony inside.

"Hey!" Tony protested as he stumbled across the floor, barely managing to stay on his feet. Harold slammed the door as Tony dropped one of the crutches. The look in Harold's eyes was the look of an insane man. He grabbed Tony by the throat and threw him up against the wall. His feet dangled, his face turning beet red.

"You little fucking weasel!" Harold shouted, spraying spittle in his face. "Only me and you knew anything. Am I right? I know I didn't tell anyone. Do you have any idea how my name came up in an investigation? Or why I was questioned by a Detective Hill from the Sheriffs Department. A damn Sergeant from Anne Arundel County Sheriff's Department?"

"You're choking me, mutha fucker!" Tony choked out, grabbing Harold's hands in his own.

Harold released his hold on the smaller man.

As Tony struggled to catch his breath, he mumbled, "I don't know."

"Wrong answer!" Harold replied, backhanding him.

"Cock sucker!" Tony yelped, feeling his lip split as blood filled his mouth. With wide eyes he wiped the blood from his mouth with the back of his right hand. "What the fuck? Give me a minute here. I need to think." Using both hands he balanced on a single crutch.

"I want some answers!" Harold demanded, raising his hand to strike him again.

"Who is the asshole you hired that fucked things up?"

"A guy I worked with in construction. He's solid!"

"Did you tell him my name?"

"Hell no! I swear I didn't. I gave him Jeff's name and told him he worked at Bethlehem Steel. I told him he was boning a friend's wife, but I didn't give him your name. I swear I didn't."

"How did he find out where Jeff lived?"

"He's got his sources. I don't ask those kind of questions."

"If you didn't tell him my name, who did you tell?" Harold asked, grabbing Tony by the throat and slamming him up against the wall for a second time.

"Nobody." Tony swore, gasping for air. "I didn't tell nobody!"

"I could crush your larynx and you would suffocate before anyone found you. Think about that, my friend. The next time I see you I want my money back and the name and address of the guy that screwed this up. Is that clear?"

"Crystal." Tony replied faintly.

When Harold released his grip Tony fell to the floor gasping for a breath of air. Harold calmly walked out of the office, closing the door behind him. It took several minutes for Tony to regain his composure.

"Mutha fucker," he cursed. He wondered what he had ever done in his miserable life to warrant such bad karma. There was no friggin' way that Domonic was going to give Harold his money back. He knew better than to even ask. He did not have the money and it was not his debt to pay.

* * *

"You want what?" Charlie asked.

"I need my twelve hundred dollar monthly child support payment." Nicole replied with a sense of urgency.

After her meeting with Hill, she had immediately returned to Charlie's apartment.

"That's history, sweetheart. You are no longer entitled to that."

"I need the money, Charlie. It's all I have to live on."

"Sorry, baby. The pussy's good, but it ain't that good," he grinned.

"You son of a bitch! Maybe Sergeant Hill was right."

"Right about what?" Charlie asked, demanding an explanation.

"Maybe you had something to do with Charlotte getting run over? Maybe you didn't want to pay child support anymore? You didn't attend her funeral. How do I know for sure that you were in Florida?"

"When did this conversation take place?" Charlie snarled, his eyes showing a dark side. A side she had never seen before.

"This afternoon. We met for coffee at the White Coffee Pot." Nicole sat on the floor, crossed her legs, and tried to change the subject. "Do you think I've got duck feet?"

Without further thought, an enraged Charlie grabbed Nicole by her hair, pulled her to her feet, opened the front door of his apartment and tossed her out into the hallway like a ragdoll. He grabbed her purse and car keys from the kitchen table and tossed them out and slammed the door shut. Nicole sat on the cold concrete floor and bursts into tears. She never knew that Charlie could be so cold hearted. This was a side of him that she had never seen before. If she had a gun, she knew she would shoot the bastard.

Nicole gathered her thoughts and her things from the ground, slowly making her way down to the parking lot and her car. Wiping away her tears with the back of her hand she climbed into the yellow Bug, started the engine, and drove to her house on Dupont Avenue in Blossom Hills. Careful to avoid driving over the spot where Charlotte was murdered, she pulled into the driveway, and parked. Then she walked out into the street where her baby had died, fell to her knees, and shed tears of anguish. She paid no attention to the various neighbors that exited their homes to console her. She cried until their were no more tears left in her. Finally, she stood, thanking the many neighbors for their concern. She stood there praying for a speeding car to come over the hill and take her life. When that failed to happen, she cursed God for making her endure so much pain.

The next morning, Nicole flipped through the Yellow pages until she found a business that bought and sold used furniture. She called and asked if they would come to her house today and make an offer for all of the furnishings, including the televisions, dishwasher, and washer and dryer. Two hours later the dealer offered her nine hundred dollars for everything. Even though the furniture was worth four times that amount, she took the money. After packing some clothes and personal items, she took a last look in Charlotte's room. Then she walked across the street and told the elderly lady she was welcome to take anything left in the house.

"Thank you," the elderly neighbor smiled. Nicole noticed that she was still wearing the blue robe and her hair was in pink curlers. She wondered how long it would be before she stopped thinking about that damn blue robe and pink curlers. She wondered if Dave had seen her neighbor up close. Her big nose, toothless smile, blackheads and wrinkles should have given him nightmares.

* * *

Tony called Harold at his home, using the pay phone from the bar. Marsha answered the phone and asked who was calling.

"Ralph, from work." Tony answered.

"Phone call, honey. Ralph, from work."

"Hello." Harold said, picking up the phone. "I need to see you now." Tony said flatly.

"Yeah, Ralph. Good looking out, it slipped my mind. I'll be right over."

"I forgot." Harold told Marsha. "I promised to help move some furniture. It shouldn't take very long," he kissed Marsha, gave her a pat on the ass, smiled, and walked out the door.

She heard the door to his black Bronco slam, the engine start and the roar of the dual exhaust as he hurried down the street.

Harold was pissed! How many times did he have to tell Tony not to call his house, explaining that his phone might be monitored. After his being questioned, there was an even greater chance of that happening.

* * *

Tony parked at the curb of the Blue Onion and waited for Harold to arrive. When Harold pulled up, Tony walked to his driver's door. Harold rolled down the window and Tony told him they had a meeting with the guy that took the hit. They were going to get his money back. But he wants to talk face to face so they could try to make sense of what happened with the police coming around.

For a brief second Harold stared at the other man, wondering if he was trying to set him up. But just as quickly as the thought entered his head, he denied that it could be possible. To him, Tony was nothing more than a coward.

"Follow me," Tony ordered.

Twenty minutes later, they drove down a secluded road in Baltimore County. Tony pulled over to the side of a graveled road and Harold pulled in behind him. Tony got out of his car and walked back to Harold.

"Park your car over there," he pointed to the other side of the road, "and ride the rest of the way with me."

Harold pulled the Bronco to the side of the road and parked in the grass. He locked the doors and climbed out to walk towards Tony, who stood in the street. A light breeze blew across his face as he watched in sudden alarm as Tony reached under his jacket and pulled out a large Colt .45 automatic. The motion had been quick and smooth.

"You wanted your friggin' money back. Here's a quarter!" Tony grinned, as he pulled the trigger. The first bullet hit Harold in the middle of his chest, and he stumbled backwards with a large blood stain darkening the front of his blue jacket.

"Here's another quarter," he squeezed the trigger a second time. "That's fifty cents." Tony said smugly.

Harold fell to the pavement, life leaking from his eyes. Tony moved to stand over him. A twisted smile crossed his face as he continued to fire round after round into the prone figure. He shot Harold four times in the chest and twice in the head, then grinning said. "That's a buck fifty you mother fucker. I guess I gotta owe you the rest."

Tony walked calmly away from the pooling blood, hopped into his car, and drove back to the Blue Onion, his problem solved.

* * *

"Baltimore County Sheriff's Department," the switchboard operator answered.

"There's a body laying in the middle of the road off Old Center-line road."

"Excuse me, Sir. Did you say a body. As in a person?"

"Yes, a white male with multiple gunshot wounds."

"Off old Centerline Road?"

"That's correct."

"What's your name, Sir?"

"Paul Estep. I live about a quarter mile down the road. I heard the gunshots, thought it was probably some kids target practicing. The little shitheads do it all the time. Didn't think nothing more about it until I drove past. There's also a empty black Ford Bronco parked at the side of the road. Man, there sure was a lot of blood."

"Did you get the license plate number?"

"No Ma'am, I hurried home to call the police."

"Sir, could you go back to ensure no one disturbs the area until the police arrive?"

"Of course."

Within minutes, the Baltimore County Sheriffs Department arrived in mass at the scene, sirens blazing and engines racing. The road was quickly roped off with yellow tape as the word spread that a brutal murder had taken place. The crime scene investigators and detectives soon followed.

Within the hour, a pair of detectives was at Marsha Bennett's front door notifying her of her husbands death.

"Are you sure," she asked, standing in the doorway of her home looking confused. "My husband left a little over an hour ago to help a friend from work move some furniture."

"I'm sorry, Ma'am," the senior of the two detectives spoke sadly. "His vehicle, a black Bronco registered to him, was found parked in the grass on the side of old Center line Road. He was identified by the photo on his driver's license."

"Oh, my God," she covered her mouth with a suddenly shaky

hand. "How did he die?"

"Your husband was shot and killed. If you need anything. If there's anything we can do."

Marsha burst into tears, her legs going weak as she slid down to the floor to hug herself in her anguish.

CHAPTER SIX
NICOLE'S WRATH

"Place a call to the Department of Motor Vehicles and see if you can get me an address for Nicole Redman's husband, Charlie Redman," Sergeant Hill instructed one of the junior detectives. Hopefully, he has a driver's license. If that doesn't work, contact the Gas and Electric Company or AT&T. I'm sure he has a telephone. He shouldn't be all that difficult to find."

Twenty six minutes later, the junior detective returned beaming with pride. "Here you go Sarge. Charlie Redman's address and phone number."

Detective Hill inspected the handwritten information. Charlie Redman lived in the Greenwood apartments in the suburbs of Glen Burnie. He noted that it was less than a ten minute's drive away. The phone number was 735-2376. Then, on a sudden impulse, he searched through the papers scattered across his desk, searching for the number the switchboard operator had given him that Nicole had called from. He quickly compared the two numbers. "Shit," he cursed under his breath. They were the same.

Instead of calling Charlie, he decided to knock on the apartment door and surprise him. Besides, he secretly wanted to see for himself what Nicole's ex-husband looked like.

On the drive over to Charlie's apartment, Hill wished he had done his homework just a little better. He wondered if his anger at the senseless death of Charlotte was starting to cloud his judgment. As he drove into the parking lot of the apartment complex, he wondered which vehicle was Charlie's, or if his car was even in the parking lot. He realized that he did not know Charlie's age, and he should have run a more detailed background check on him before leaving the station.

He began to wonder if Charlie had a criminal history as a juvenile or adult. About the only thing he knew for certain was that Nicole had called from Charlie's apartment, and for some reason he was sorely irritated by it. Even though he knew he had no right to be. He was glad to see her car was not in the parking lot. It was at that moment he realized he was acting out of jealousy. But he could not seem to help himself, and not that it seemed to matter in the course of his job. Not at the moment anyway.

He parked the car in the half filled parking lot between a pickup truck and a Dodge van. Exiting the car, he slammed the door. Hurrying across the paved parking lot, he took the metal stairs two at a time up to the second floor. He went past four doors before arriving at Charlie's apartment. He knocked calmly on the door.

"Whatever you're selling, I'm not interested." Charlie snapped, answering the door.

"I'm not selling anything." Sergeant Hill replied, quickly displaying his badge with his right hand before replacing it back inside his suits bottom jacket pocket. He leaned against the door and looked over Charlie's shoulder and into his apartment. He failed to see Nicole, but he did not expect to. Especially since her car was not there.

"My name is Detective Sergeant Hill and I'm with the Sheriffs Department. We're investigating the death of your daughter, Charlotte."

"Oh yeah, Nicole mentioned you. She said you think I might have had something to do with our daughter's death?" Charlie's anger was plain to see on his face. He was of average height and thin as a rail. His hair was dark, curly, and covered his rather large ears.

"May I come in?"

"Hell no! Since I'm a suspect, if you want to talk to me, call my attorney." Charlie walked back into the apartment and over to his kitchen table, and picked up a business card. He returned to the door and handed it to the detective. "That's my attorney's number. Give him a call."

"So, you're going to lawyer up on me, huh?"

"That's right," he smiled, then added. "If you should happen to see that bitch ex-wife of mine, would you tell her that my attorney assures me that I no longer have to pay child support. The bitch wanted me to give her twelve hundred bucks!"

"Did you?"

"Fuck no! I told her the pussy was good, but not that good," Charlie laughed.

Sergeant Hill looked at him for a long moment, briefly thought about punching him in his smug face. Instead he glanced around, and satisfied that there were no eye witnesses, he grabbed Charlie's head and slammed it against the door. Charlie gave a yelp of surprise, in no serious pain.

"You've got to be careful around those damn door frames," Hill grinned.

Charlie felt his head, then he looked at his hand to see if there was any blood. There was nothing but a small lump maturing on the left side of his throbbing head. "Assault, assault!" Charlie shouted, but there was no one around. If anyone heard the thud they chose not to show themselves. No doors opened and no one came running to his rescue.

Detective Hill grinned and calmly walked away, disappointed with Nicole's taste in men. Charlie had not been much to look at and Hill wondered what in the name of Sam's Hell did Nicole see in him in the first place. Deep down, he knew there was no connection between Charlie and Charlotte's death. The truth was he knew before he ever made the trip to Charlie's apartment! The connection between the assault, the stolen vehicle and Charlotte's death was pretty much a sure thing. He needed to put his personal feelings aside. Sadly enough, he was doing a piss poor job of doing that.

He drove down Mountain road to Blossom Hills and then by Nicole's house. From the street, he could see there were no curtains in the windows and the house was vacant. Where was Nicole now, he wondered? He drove another three blocks to Sharonville and stopped to see Vivian Miles. He probably should have been more considerate and called first, but this was not a planned trip. While he was in the area and on the spur of the moment, it seemed like a good time to interview the woman who reported the car parked on the grass the morning Jeff was assaulted. Perhaps if she was shown a photo of the stolen blue Pontiac Bonneville, she would positively identify it. At least, that's what he hoped for.

Vivian Miles graciously pointed out where the neighbor lived, as well as where she said the car had been parked.

Detective Hill thanked her, walked to the neighbors house, and knocked on the door. There was no answer.

* * *

Detective Marks was just arriving at the office. He parked his Cadillac Coupe Deville in the employee parking lot, pulled a fresh cigar from his shirt pocket, bit off the tip, spit it on the ground and flipped open his Zippo lighter. With a flick of his thumb, there was a spark, and cigar smoke filled the air. He made his way across the parking lot to the station.

Everyone in the office hated the smell of his stinking cigars, but no one ever dared complain. Amongst themselves they joked that with his big belly and rosy red cheeks, he looked like Jackie Gleason, the actor. The difference being he lacked any personality. Detective Marks was a no nonsense, straight to the point kind of guy. As he walked into the office, and before he could grab a cup of coffee, check his messages, or sit down at his desk, he was rushed by junior detectives hoping to gain favoritism.

"Sheila Watts was born…"

"Hold it right there!" Detective Marks said sternly, holding up the palm of his hand. "Save it! In thirty minutes we are going to all meet in the conference room where we will openly share information and take notes."

"Yes, Sir," came the reply.

Thirty minutes later, everyone gathered in the conference room with their coffee, writing pads and pens. Each of them placed a file folder on the table in front of them.

"Okay," Marks began. "From left to right, beginning with Greg, give me a report on what you have. There's no reason to repeat information that has already been given. Does everyone understand?"

"Yes," the detectives answered in unison.

"Greg, what do you have?"

"Sheila Watts was born September ninth, nineteen forty two at Saint Joseph's Hospital in Baltimore, Maryland. Her mother's maiden name was Harriet Stump. She died when Sheila was twelve. Her father's name is Matthew Watts. He's a retired railroad worker. At this time his address is unknown."

"Wyatt, do you have anything to add," Marks addressed the next man in line.

"Yes, Sir, Missy was twenty-six years old with blonde hair and blue eyes. My informant says that she was a well known prostitute."

"Is that it?"

"Yes, Sir."

"You're up next, Ronnie." Detective Marks said, taking a sip of coffee.

"Sheila's last known boyfriend was in High School. Ronnie Scott escorted her to the junior prom. My source tells me that she was bisexual, and that she preferred having relationships with girls."

"And how would that information aid in this investigation?" Marks growled.

"Sir, I believe everyone is assuming the killer was a man. That may not be true."

"Good point, Twinkle Toes. Have you anything you wish to add to this College of shared information?" Detective Marks called Betty Crawford 'Twinkle Toes' because of her polished toenails that were exposed at the tip of her high-heeled shoes. Being from the old school of cops, he thought a woman's place was in the household, or occupying a desk. This made him feel an obligation to look after Twinkle Toes.

Betty Crawford felt the nickname to be degrading. Yet she never complained or made her feelings known, instead she sucked it up, and smiled pleasantly.

"Missy's father Matthew lives at fifteen eighty-seven Reistertown Road in Reistertown, Maryland. He is seventy-two years old and his home number is ninety-four one thirty thirtyone. I went to the residence and notified him of his daughter's death, then made an appointment to interview him at one O'clock this afternoon. My informants confirm that Missy was a known prostitute. She primarily worked along the strip of Baltimore street. She also frequented several after-hour clubs, noticeably the Wee Hours at the corner of Fleet and Broadway. Missy worked for two brothers, Dick and Jerry Everhart. They have been arrested three times for pandering. They also own an after-hour club downtown. It's called Hectors."

"Does anyone have a lead on who made the emergency call?" Everyone shook their heads, acknowledging they knew nothing. Detective Marks twirled the cigar in his mouth, made a funny face, then reported, "Good job, Twinkle Toes." It was said regretfully. Then he added, "I'll go with you on the interview."

* * *

AT&T received requests from two different police districts requesting a copy of the monthly billing of the Bennett residence. At that point an AT&T supervisor made both districts aware of the separate request. Based on this information Hill discovered that Harold Bennett had been brutally gunned down and a Detective Daniels from the Baltimore County Sheriff's Department was the name of other detective making the request. Sergeant Hill narrowed his request by asking 'specifically' for calls made to the Bennett residence on the night of the murder. Also, he asked for those calls to be made available immediately.

It was a couple hours later when he received the billing. He immediately noted there was only one incoming call which lasted for less than two minutes. Actually, closer to one minute. That had to be the call he was searching for! AT&T showed the call to originate from a pay phone at 621 Howard Street. Sergeant Hill soon discovered the address was a business called the Blue Onion. He chuckled to himself. Who would be foolish enough to name a bar the Blue Onion?

A detective stuck his head in Hill's office, smiled and said, "There's a call for you on line four."

Hill shooed him out of his office. He thought about answering with a, "Hi Nicole," but resisted the temptation in case he was wrong. He hoped she would call. He expected her to call.

"Hello," he answered.

"Sergeant Hill?"

"This is Vivian Miles. I thought you might want to know Jeff is having difficulty breathing, even with a respirator. The doctor asked if I wanted to continue to keep him on life support."

"Have you made a decision?"

"Not yet. It's so hard!" Vivian replied and broke down crying.

"Is there any thing I can do to help?"

"I don't think so…

"Will you be going to the hospital tonight?"

"I go every night around six o' clock."

"I'll see you there."

"Okay," Vivian said, quietly hanging up the phone.

Sergeant Hill was pretty certain that he would soon have three murders to solve, knowing by the sound of things that Jeff Miles was not long for this world. First there was little Charlotte Redman. Then Harold Bennett and finally there would be Jeff Miles. The bodies were piling up and complicating the investigation more and more with each passing second. Knowing how important it was for him to stay on top of the investigation, he headed back to the office, hoping for a break in the case sometime real soon.

* * *

There were well over a hundred cars in the funeral procession for Harold Bennett. Most were employees from Bethlehem Steel. Union workers from Local 431. They were there to pay their respects and offer condolences to Harold's wife, Marsha Bennett. Marsha and her five children stood alongside the casket as the eulogy was given. "Ashes to ashes and dust to dust…" Megan, their youngest daughter wrapped her little arms around Marsha's leg. She cried, then asked, "Momma, what happened to Daddy?" Marsha looked down with a sad smile. "God has called your father home, honey. I know you don't understand, but someday you will." Marsha kissed Megan on the top of her head and ran her fingers through her hair.

Sergeant Hill offered Marsha his condolences and promised to call her in a few days.

* * *

"Charlie!" Nicole screamed, beating her fists on the door of his apartment. "I know you're in there asshole, and you better give me my clothes!"

Nicole had tried calling, to no avail. Charlie's Corvette Stingray was in the parking lot, so she knew he was there.

Inside the apartment Charlie awoke, startled by a loud pounding on the door. His head throbbed, suffering a hangover from Hell. He was mentally and physically exhausted by a hard night of partying. Rolling over he looked at the naked girl laying beside him. One leg, and her bare ass, was hanging out of the covers. Charlie wondered who she was? From a pile of discarded clothing on the floor he grabbed his boxer shorts, put them on, closed the bed room door behind him, and headed for the front door flinching every time someone pounded on it.

He peered through the peephole before opening the door.

"I just want my clothes." Nicole hurriedly said, her right foot tapping impatiently on the ground. She looked at his swollen head. It was black and blue on the left side.

"What happened to you," she frowned.

"Your boyfriend paid me a visit."

"I don't have a boyfriend," she retorted.

"Your cop boyfriend." Charlie snapped, wishing he had a cigarette.

"Dave," she frowned.

"I don't know his fucking name. He's lucky I didn't have him arrested."

"Why did he hit you?"

"We had a few words. I told him what you said about my being a possible suspect in Charlotte's murder. He wanted to come inside, and I wouldn't let him. Instead of agreeing to talk, I referred him to my lawyer. He got upset and made some wisecrack about my lawyering up on him. When I told him that I refused to give you any money because your pussy wasn't that good, he slammed my head against the fucking door."

Nicole smiled broadly, suddenly pleased to see him hurt and suffering. "Well, I just came to get the rest of my things."

"It's not a good time. I have company," Charlie pleaded.

"Give me a eight ball of cocaine and I'll come back later," Nicole offered.

"That's extortion!" Charlie snapped.

"So!" Nicole laughed. "I'll go away quietly. It's your choice."

A few minutes later Nicole left quietly.

* * *

Sergeant Hill left the office and drove immediately home. Hill turned the key in the front door to his apartment, walked directly into the kitchen, opened the refrigerator, and grabbed a cold beer before going to switch on the television. Just as he took a seat in a recliner, the phone on the end table beside the chair rang.

"Hello," he answered.

"Did you beat up Charlie?"

"Nicole? How did you get my phone number?"

"You're not the only one who can be resourceful," she laughed, then asked again," Did you beat up Charlie?"

"Not exactly," he chuckled, and took a swig of beer.

"Yes, you did!" Nicole giggled. "You're my knight in shining armor. Where is your white horse?"

"Where are you? I drove past your house, it's vacant."

"I sold everything and moved."

"Where did you move to?"

"You're a cop, find me!"

"Seriously Nicole, we need to talk. Have you heard what happened to Harold Bennett?"

"No, what happened?"

"Can you meet me at the White Coffee Pot, in say, half an hour?"

"I'll be there!"

When Sergeant Hill arrived Nicole had once again beaten him there. Her yellow Volkswagen was parked in front of the restaurant. He spotted her sitting in a booth, looking out the window, as he parked his Maverick. Nicole smiled as he walked inside and sat down.

"I ordered you a coffee. One cream and two sugars," she said smiling, proud of herself for remembering that about him.

Sergeant Hill briefly shared her smile. He shook his head, then reported. "Harold Bennett was murdered. I just attended his funeral this afternoon."

"How did it happen?"

"According to his wife he received a call the day of his death. The caller identified himself as Ralph. Harold told his wife that he had forgot having promised to help a friend from work move some furniture. He gave her a kiss and quickly left his house. Three hours later two Baltimore County detectives knocked on the door and informed her of her husband's death. His black Bronco was found parked near his body on old Centerline Road in Baltimore County. Harold was left laying in a pool of blood in the middle of the street. He had been shot six times. The call was made from a bar on Howard Street. A place called the Blue Onion."

"Did he have any children?"

"Five."

"God, that's terrible. How is his wife taking it?"

"She's a strong woman, I've got to be at the North Arundel Hospital in thirty minutes. I'm meeting Vivian Miles there. Her husband's condition has gone from bad to worse and she has to make a tough decision. She has to decide whether to keep her husband on life support, or not."

"I'm going with you," Nicole insisted.

* * *

Detective Hill introduced the two women, then explained. "Vivian, Nicole wanted to meet you. It was her daughter who was run over by the stolen car."

"I'm so sorry!" Vivian said, embracing Nicole.

Hill let the two women have a moment to share in their grief. He knew that he could no longer keep the truth from Vivian. Especially now that there was, more than likely, a link between Jeff's assault and the murder of Harold Bennett. He had to tell Vivian about Jeff's affair with Harold Bennett's wife. There were just too many unanswered questions.

Vivian was shocked to hear of her husband's infidelity. Even more upset when she was told that Marsha Bennett was a Call Girl.

Nicole and Hill spent the required time helping Vivian cope with her newfound grief. When they finally left, both of them were feeling emotionally drained.

A few minutes later, when the doctor entered the room and asked Vivian if she was able to make a decision. Vivian stood over Jeff, looked her husband in the face, and thought she saw a flicker of movement. "Pull the plug!"

She refused to have a husband who cheated on her!

* * *

Detective Marks and Betty Crawford interviewed Sheila Watts' father, Matthew. Betty dreaded going anywhere with her boss. He always insisted they go in his car. He was a horrible driver, and the smell of his damn cigars was overwhelming. Putting it bluntly, they stunk!

Matthew 'Matt' Watts hadn't seen or spoken to his daughter in eleven years. Missy quit school and moved out of the house when she turned sixteen.

Hopefully, when they interviewed Dick and Jerry Everhart, they would pick up a lead. However, since the brothers were the only suspects they had in the case, a decision was made not to interview them.

The question looming in everyone's mind was, who placed the emergency phone call.

* * *

It was eight o' clock at night when Sergeant Hill dropped Nicole off at her car. They spoke for a few minutes, then he drove to his apartment. As he turned into the parking lot, he glanced in his rearview mirror. Nicole' s yellow Bug was behind him with the big amber turn signal flashing on the left fender. He quickly parked, shaking his head in disbelief, and walked over to her car. She rolled her window down, looking at him with a smile and said. "So this is where you live?"

"What are you doing, Nicole?"

She laughed. "Do you wanna get lucky? You can use your hand-cuffs on me."

"I'm a cop. This is very unprofessional."

"Shut up, Dave. It's no wonder you never get laid!"

"Who says I never get laid? My personal life is none of your business."

"Which apartment is yours?"

"The messy one. I haven't had time to clean it lately."

"I know you've got some beer in there," Nicole smiled.

"I've got beer," he said, thinking she had such a beautiful smile. How could anyone say no to her? "I don't suppose it would do me any good to tell you no?"

"You can say whatever you want, but I'm going to do whatever I want. I have a mind of my own. Keep that in mind." Nicole smiled, as she climbed out of the car and followed him to his apartment. While driving she took time to switch from wearing tennis shoes to flip-flops. Her toenails were freshly polished a bright pink.

When they entered the apartment her eyes roamed freely. It was a one bedroom apartment on the first floor, facing the parking lot. Dirty dishes were piled high in the tiny kitchen. Clothes littered the living room. It was a man's cave, she concluded.

Sergeant Hill opened the door to his refrigerator and said, "I only have Budweiser. Is that okay?"

"That's fine. Where's your bathroom?"

"Down the hall, first door on the right." He pointed towards a short hallway off to the right side of the kitchen.

As she headed down the hall, she came abreast of the open bathroom door. Directly in front of her she noticed a partially open door. A mirror on a dresser caught her eye. The mirror reflected a wall with a closet, the sliding doors open displaying an array of shirts, pants, and jackets hanging from hangers. She walked into his bedroom and grabbed a shirt from its hanger.

First door on the right? She mused. There was only two doors! His bedroom and the bathroom. A short time later she walked from the bathroom wearing his long sleeve shirt, the shirt tail falling down to her knees. The sleeves were rolled up and she was naked underneath.

He looked up, smiled shyly at the sight of her, then extended his hand, offering her a beer.

"That's the best you've got to offer me," she giggled, starting to open the shirt from the top one button at a time.

"Nicole…"

She placed a finger over his mouth and reminded him. "You said you like your women hot and sassy."

A sudden passion consumed him. He grabbed her ass using his left hand, kissing her passionately, while running his right hand up her shirt front. She quickly finished unbuttoning the shirt, exposing small but well rounded tits. She fought desperately to rid him of his shirt, and soon they felt the warmth of bare skin. He unbuckled his pants giving her access to caress and pull on his manhood. First they made love with her sitting on his lap in the Lazy Boy recliner. Next on the kitchen counter, and then finally in his bed. His hunger for her was like none he had never known before and it scared him.

At midnight, he left her asleep in the bed, dressed, and left his apartment to go to the Blue Onion. He wanted to interview people before the Baltimore County Sheriffs Department got involved. He wanted the first shot at questioning witnesses.

As the apartment door closed, Nicole awoke from a horrific nightmare. In the dream a dark blue Pontiac Bonneville was backing up and running over her daughter again and again, all while Charlotte Lynn screamed. "Help me, mommy! Help me mommy!"

Nicole sat up in the bed, tears of anguish streaming down her face; the unfamiliar surroundings suddenly all too frightening. When she did get her bearing, she called into the dark room. "Dave! Dave!"

She reached for the lamp next to bed and turned it on. She was heart-broken, and Dave was nowhere be found. She looked for a note.

There was none. She dressed, She then spent an hour cleaning the apartment. He still had not returned. She wrote a note, stuck it to the refrigerator with a magnet, and walked out the door.

Nicole stopped at an all night Pharmacy. She bought some platinum blonde hair dye, returned to her efficiency apartment, dyed her hair and cut it in a Pixie. She had one purpose in life…to find Charlotte's murderer. Whatever it took, she swore revenge.

CHAPTER SEVEN
THE BLUE ONION

The door to the Blue Onion was once again propped open. Tony stood just outside the door, collecting the two dollar coverage charge as patron's entered the bar. In between the door collecting the arrival of each patron, he rolled a quarter through his fingers. When Sergeant Hill showed up and tried to walk through the door, Tony extended his arm across the threshold of the door blocking his entrance.

"There's a two dollar cover charge."

Sergeant Hill flashed his badge, looking past his arm into the crowded bar. The music was thumping loud, while voices were raised in celebration. He could clearly see a dyed blonde humping away on top of the bar, her tits bare for the world to see.

"There's still a two dollar cover charge..." Tony grinned.

"I'm here on official business..."

"I'm the manager," Tony announced, "and I didn't call for any assistance."

"This is a murder investigation."

"A murder? Some of these girls dance and fuck like they're dead. Some even smell like dead fish, but they're all still breathing," Tony chuckled.

"Do you have a place where we can talk in private." Detective Hill asked, trying to maintain his professionalism.

Tony called a big burley bouncer from inside the bar. "Watch the door," he instructed.

He led Hill inside the dimly lit bar, through the carousing crowd, and back to the rear office. Unlocking the door he led him inside.

"Do you know a Harold Bennett?" Sergeant Hill got right down to business.

"The name doesn't ring a bell. If I had a nickel for every guy that walked through the door, I could retire. Why? Did he kill someone?"

"No, he was murdered. He was found laying in the middle of a road in Baltimore County in a pool of blood."

"What does that have to do with this bar?"

"The last call made to his house was from a pay phone here. Harold's wife took the call. The caller identified himself as Ralph. Harold supposedly left to go help move some furniture. Half an hour later he was dead."

"What Department are you with?"

"I'm with the Anne Arundel County Sheriffs Department."

"Anne Arundel County? Aren't you out of your friggin' jurisdiction? This is Baltimore City and you said the murder occurred in Baltimore County."

"I think it's tied to an assault that took place against a Jeff Miles." Sergeant Hill said hoping to get a response from the other man. His face remained blank. "A six year old girl was run over during the get away. She died instantly."

Tony failed to hide the visible flinch around his mouth and eyes. "Why didn't you ask if I knew Jeff Miles," he tried to cover his sudden nervousness.

Hill caught the tightening around his eyes. "Do you?"

"Nope!" Tony rolled the quarter through his fingers, flipped it into the air, then caught it.

"Do you mind if I interview the girls?"

"As long as you pay the two dollar cover charge, you can ask them anything you want."

Sergeant Hill reached into his wallet and begrudgingly handed Tony two one dollar bills. Once again he realized that he was unprepared. He should have brought a photo of Harold to show the girls. He seriously doubted that any of the girls knew the names of guys they hustled, but they would remember their faces.

After talking with the girls, he left. He had learned nothing, but his gut was telling him that Tony knew much more than he was saying. When he arrived home, he found the apartment had been cleaned from front to back. Going into the bedroom, the bed was empty and neatly made. Nicole was gone. He walked back to the kitchen and as he started to open the door to the refrigerator, he saw the note. It read, "Fuck you!"

"Damnit!" Hill cursed, grabbing a cold beer from the refrigerator. He returned to the bedroom. Laying on the bed he smelled her scent and longed to put his arms around her.

* * *

Having sold everything of value, Nicole's efficiency apartment had no television or radio. Alone with her thoughts she grabbed her purse, opened it, and pulled out the eight ball of cocaine Charlie had given her. It was wrapped in plastic, weighed, and packaged for sale. She opened the package, laid out two inch long lines, rolled up a dollar bill and snorted a line into each nostril. She tilted her head back and sniffed hard several times.

It was time for her to get down and dirty. There would be no limits! She was certain that whoever was responsible for her daughter's murder would be someone of a criminal element.

It was going to be challenging. She was going to have to learn to behave badly. To flaunt her God given assets and associate with the underbelly of the street world if she ever hoped to find Charlotte's killer. For a brief moment she had found comfort in Dave's arms. But he had left her alone to live with her nightmares. Maybe Charlie was right. He had once accused her of being too stubborn for her own good. Her mind was certainly made up.

Tomorrow she was going to talk to Marsha Bennett, because according to Dave, Marsha had heard the caller's voice. Why Dave failed to think of this was beyond her. Maybe the caller stuttered or had an accent? She would ask Marsha herself if there was a chance of her recognizing the voice if she heard it again. She had a vested interest in finding the murderer of her husband. Surely she would want her husband's killer brought to justice, even if that justice was vigilante justice. Marsha was a Call Girl with brains, having knowledge and experience, and possibly connections; things Nicole knew she would need.

Nicole was proud of her uncanny ability to remember things. She had always possessed a knack for being able to recall the smallest detail. Several years earlier she tried to go on a game show where the contestants picked squares, matching them to another square. When watching the program on television, she always remembered where they were. It was easy for her, and she laughed when the contestants failed to remember. Sometimes she yelled at the television, enjoying the show so much that she often spoke out loud as if they could hear her. Cocaine gave her a boost that helped her think deeper about things she might have otherwise overlooked, The cocaine suddenly kicked in making her feel empowered, like she was on top of the world. When in reality, she was sitting in a small efficiency apartment in Glen Burnie with no television, no radio, and no phone.

"When life hands you lemons, make lemonade." Nicole said to herself reaching for the plastic baggy of cocaine. She laid out two lines, and snorted one into each nostril. Then she sniffed hard several times.

* * *

"Son of a bitch, we just can't ever get a break!" Detective Marks snarled.

His request for a wire tap on Dick and Jerry Everhart's after-hour club and home was denied. The judge felt there was insufficient evidence to grant the warrant. There simply was no probable cause! Marks felt it was a hard blow to the investigation. His plan had been to interview the Everharts to rattle the bushes and hope something useful fell out. In most cases, people's first reaction was to pick up a phone and make a call within minutes after being interviewed. They always called someone. Someone involved, a confident, a best friend, or their attorney.

"Damn that judge!" One of the junior detectives shouted angrily. Emotions were running high.

Detective Marks grinned, looked at the junior detective, and explained. "Son, suspicion doesn't amount to reason to believe, much less meet the standard of probable cause. It was a shot in the dark. I was hoping the judge would simply look over the application for the search warrant and sign it. Today he actually took the time to read it," Detective Marks chuckled.

"What now?" Betty Crawford asked.

"How well do you know your informant? And just how well does he or she know Dick and Jerry Everhart?"

"My informant is a he. I can ask him."

"While you're at it, ask him if he would be willing to wear a wire?"

Betty Crawford smiled, then quickly left the room. Detective Marks eyes followed her as she walked away. She was wearing a tight fitting black skirt and a white blouse with lace around the collar. Her jet black hair fell to her shoulders, except when she tied it in a ponytail, which was most of the time; just not today. Today her hair was stunningly attractive. She never wore makeup and her black rimmed glasses did nothing to compliment her many assets. By God, he thought, she really does have a beautiful body. One that could stop traffic! It was difficult not to stare at her hips and ass when she turned to exit a room, and frankly why would anyone want to look in any other direction?

If the informant could be trusted, and agreed to wearing a wire, it could be their best chance to obtaining any substantial evidence. They were running out of options. At least their Jane Doe corpse finally had a name. Sheila 'Missy' Watts.

* * *

Bethlehem Steel telephoned Vivian Miles. Extending their condolences, they offered to pay for her husband's funeral.

"My husband is going to be cremated." Vivian replied, thanking the caller for the offer. She would not put herself, or her children through another moment of grief. Not on his account. Vivian reserved the sympathy for herself. Jeff had cheated on her, and left her to raise two children by herself.

* * *

Nicole went to Greenlawn cemetery to visit her daughter's grave. Getting down on her knees, she used her hands to brush dirt from the headstone. She placed a single rose on top of the grave, then took a few moments to pick the few weeds that had grown up around the headstone.

"I'm so sorry, baby. Momma should have never allowed you to play in the street. I hope you can forgive me for not protecting you better. I love and miss you so much, and Momma's going to find the man responsible for hurting you. You probably already know that he stole a car and assaulted a man with a baseball bat. I'm sure that you probably already know who he is. I'm going to find him and hold him accountable for what he's done. That's a promise, baby!" Nicole said a silent prayer, pleading with God to take good care of her baby.

After she left the cemetery, Nicole stopped at a phone booth and looked through the directory until she found the name of Harold Bennett. His address was 1402 Patapasco Avenue. The phone number, 328-9002. Nicole dug deep into the pocket of her tight fitting Levi's for change. She inserted a dime into the coin slot, listened for a dial tone, then dialed the number.

"Hello?" the voice on the other end answered.

"Hello. My name is Nicole Redman. You don't know me, but I'm the mother of the little girl that was killed by a car believed to be linked to the assault of Jeff Miles. I'm sorry about the murder of your husband, but I need your help!"

"My help?" Marsha said, sounding confused.

"Yes, I believe there's a connection between all of these events."

"The authorities are investigating that." Marsha replied coldly.

"The authorities aren't doing jack shit!" Nicole snapped, "They labeled my daughter's murder a hit and run accident. She was murdered!"

"I'm sorry for your loss. But there's nothing I can do to help you."

"Just give me ten minutes of your time. We can have a cup of coffee, and I promise I will leave you alone."

"I'm sorry," Marsha replied and hung up the phone.

Nicole dug deep in her pocket for another dime and dialed the number right back.

Marsha answered the phone, heard her voice, and hung right up.

"You bitch!" Nicole cursed, slamming the receiver in its cradle. She stopped at a gas station, filled the gas tank, and while she waited asked the attendant for directions to Patapasco Avenue.

Twenty minutes later she parked at the curb in front of Marsha Bennett's red brick ranch style home. A white Mustang convertible was parked in the driveway. Nicole assumed the car to be Marsha's. She quickly hopped out of the Bug, scurried across the front lawn and up to the closed front screen door. She began pounding on the door with closed fists.

"You're going to talk to me bitch," she screamed.

The front door was suddenly yanked open. Marsha stood there, then calmly unlocked the screen door, opened it, and looked Nicole up and down. "You don't take no for an answer, do you? How do you like your coffee?" Marsha asked, smiling. She opened the door wider, inviting Nicole inside. As they entered the kitchen, Marsha motioned for her to sit down at the small kitchen table.

"I like my coffee black."

Marsha reached inside a cabinet, grabbed a mug, picked the coffee pot up from the stove, poured a cup of coffee, and handed it to Nicole.

"What's on your mind?" Marsha asked, propping a hip against the counter near the sink.

"I'm really sorry to hear about your husband."

"Harold was a good man." Marsha sighed.

"Let me get right to the point. Harold received a phone call from someone who gave the name, Ralph. You heard the caller's voice. Was there anything distinctive about it? If you heard it again would you recognize it?"

Marsha looked thoughtful for a second, then smiled. "Now that you mentioned it, I might be able to recognize his voice. He spoke like a street person. Like the gangsters in the movies."

"Did the detectives ask you the same question?"

"No. But how did you find out about the caller?"

"I have my sources," Nicole smiled.

"Don't play games with me little girl. If you want to play games, you can source your little ass right out the door you came in."

"I fucked Dave."

"Dave?" Marsha repeated, totally confused.

"Sergeant Hill."

Marsha laughed. "You're a conniving little bitch, aren't you?" As a second thought hit her, she asked. "Was he any good?"

"Great! He was well endowed, had stamina, and knew how to please me," Nicole giggled.

"What else did he tell you?"

"That you're a Call girl."

"That son of a bitch told you that?" Marsha swore. She was livid.

"Yes, he did. If you want to find out who murdered your husband, then help me." Nicole pleaded.

"How can I help you?"

"The call to your husband was placed from a pay phone at a bar on Howard street called the Blue Onion. Do you know where it is?"

"No."

"I want to place a call there tonight. I can ask to speak with the manager, claiming I'm interested in being interviewed for a job as a dancer. Maybe we can go hang out there for a couple nights to see if you recognize anyone's voice. I'm sure you know about titty dancers. You can listen in on another line to see if the manager is being straight with me."

"You're a smart cookie." Marsha agreed with a smile.

"I also want you to teach me everything you know about being a stripper, and whore. Do you know how to dance?"

"Honey I know all the moves!"

"How much do you charge for…"

"For my services?" Marsha interjected. "First off, I'm not a whore. I don't stand on street corners and turn tricks. I got into the business because Harold and I have five children. He worked hard, but there was no way we would ever be able to pay for the kids to go to college on what he was bringing home. I've been stashing money for some time now. To answer your question, I wouldn't take my shoes off for less than a hundred dollars! In some cases I make three hundred, or more. I have an appointment at Two O'Clock, and the client wants two girls. I was going to call one of my girlfriends, but if you're really serious, here's your chance to pick up a fast three hundred dollars."

"What do I have to do?"

"Whatever the client wants. This client likes to watch girl on girl action."

"I have never done that," Nicole admitted, but shocked to feel a rise of excitement at the thought.

Marsha noticed the nipples of her small tits hardening through her white T-shirt. She smiled. "It's up to you. But if you're going to play the game, you are going to need to prepare yourself for what comes with it."

"I'll do it." Marsha was attractive and Nicole sensed that she would be a good teacher.

"The blue jeans are fine, but we're going to have to find you a blouse and pair of shoes," Marsha decided, giving her the once over.

"You don't like my flip-flops?"

Marsha led the way to her large back bedroom. From the closet she selected a red blouse and a pair of red high-heels. "This should be more appropriate."

Marsha next walked to the living room with Nicole in tow, turned on the stereo, and for the next two hours, she taught Nicole how to roll her hips, shake her ass, and flow her body to the beat of the music. Watching Nicole learning how to hump an imaginary pole was hilarious, yet thrilling. On impulse Marsha leaned over to kiss Nicole full on the mouth. Without a seconds thought, Nicole returned her kiss passionately, running her tongue down Marsha's throat. Marsha pulled away with a soft chuckle.

"You'll do fine."

Marsha told Nicole to park her car in the driveway. Parking was not permitted on the street, but at the time Nicole had not cared. She didn't give a rat's ass about the rules. From now on she would be making the rules. After getting cleaned up and dressing to appear sexy, they exited the house and walked to Marsha's Mustang convertible. Marsha unlocked the doors, started the engine, then put the top down. Within minutes they were driving down the road with their hair blowing wildly in the wind. Nicole tuned the radio to her favorite station and began to sing along with the music. Marsha smiled approvingly.

The client lived in an elegant high-rise apartment building located on the tenth floor. He was slightly overweight, in his mid fifties, and he was well dressed and perfectly groomed. The apartment was large and tastefully decorated. Fine china and a silver tea server sat on top of a side table. Two large gray couches, a gray leather Lazy Boy recliner, and a white bear rug sat beneath a glassed top coffee table. Two matching glassed end tables with chrome legs were topped with elegant lamps. The carpet was white and plush, and expensive works of art covered the walls. When Nicole removed her shoes, it felt as if she was walking on balls of cotton. From the balcony there was a spectacular view overlooking the City of Baltimore.

"Nicole, this is Manny." Marsha introduced the two.

"My pleasure." Manny said, with an approving eye. "If you girls want a drink, help yourselves."

Manny excused himself, and walked down the hallway closing his bedroom door behind him. Marsha made Nicole and herself a stiff drink, Jack Daniel's whiskey and Coca-Cola with ice.

Manny returned wearing a white robe, the gray hairs on his chest exposed, and a thin gold necklace with a Saint Christopher medallion dangling from his neck. "Would you ladies care to step into the bedroom and make yourselves more comfortable?"

Marsha held out her hand, palm up. "Money first," she replied.

"Of course!" Manny smiled. He reached into the pocket of his robe and handed her six crisp one hundred dollar bills. Marsha smiled, passing over three of them to Nicole.

The trio retired to Manny's bedroom. In the middle of the room there was a round bed with white satin sheets and a red velvet headboard. Wasting no time Marsha removed her clothes down to a black g-string, which barely covered her mound. Following Marsha's lead, Nicole slowly took off her clothes, revealing that she was wearing no underwear. Her fur patch was neatly groomed, like a landing strip.

Manny smiled approvingly.

Marsha took Nicole by the hand and lain her down on the bed. She kissed her tenderly, slowly running her hand up her thigh. At the other woman's touch, Nicole felt shivers up and down her spine. Marsha was gentle except when she twisted one of Nicole's nipples between two fingers, sent sparks shooting through her body like a bolt of electricity.

Almost hungrily she began to make love to Nicole. First caressing her small breast before sucking each of them in turn.

Marsha kissed her way down Nicole's flat stomach to her belly button, her tongue tracing in slow circular motions. Once in awhile she paused, glancing at Manny for his approval. His smile was enough! Spreading Nicole's legs wide for his viewing pleasure, she inserted a finger, easing down on the bed to part the lips of her into her moist, warm, pussy. She flicked her tongue back and forth in rapid succession on her clit. Nicole moaned, wiggled her ass, and feebly tried to escape Marsha's tongue.

Nicole was shocked by the response of her body to another woman's touch. Her body was on fire as Marsha attacked her pussy steadily pumping a finger in and out of her wet pussy while skillfully flipping her clit with her tongue. Then suddenly in the throes of passion, Nicole could feel her orgasm exploding. "Oh God, yes! Yes." Her body convulsed with a feeling she had never felt before.

Marsha moved slowly back up Nicole's body to kiss her passionately, sliding her tongue deep into her mouth. After catching her breath Nicole knew it was time to turn the tables. Recalling the things Marsha had done to her, an inexperienced Nicole first kissed her, then rolled Marsha onto her back; fondling her tits and gently sucking them. They were much larger than hers, and looking at Marsha's body she could not believe that she had given birth to five children. Her body was still flawless, her breasts with barely any sag. Nicole ignored the presence of Manny who constantly paced around the bed, watching the two women in breathless delight.

Nicole climbed between Marsha's legs and inserted a finger deep into Marsha's wet pussy, moving it slowly in and out. She rubbed her moist mound, parted her lips, and suddenly leaned forward darting her tongue over Marsha's clit. Then she reached down further and shoved her wet finger into Marsha's ass, causing both her and Manny to gasp out in surprise. Marsha squirmed all over, her body trying to escape the overwhelming pleasure that Nicole was giving her, the feeling too intense. In truth she did not want to escape. Marsha moaned, cried out, and juices flowed freely from her pussy like Niagara Falls as she reached her climax. Nicole licked her lips as she rose up to stare down at Marsha. The two women shared a smile.

Manny was pleased. He thought Nicole was outstanding, young and beautiful, having never seen Marsha enjoy herself so much. He gave the girls an extra hundred dollars each and asked if he could make another appointment to see them next week.

Marsha looked to Nicole for her approval. Nicole smiled her agreement, so Marsha quickly replied. "Of course!"

They went to wash and get dressed before gathering their things, and thanking Manny for the extra money. They left the middle aged man alone with a happy smile.

When they were back in the car, Marsha stared over at Nicole in wonder. "You're something else," she giggled, while starting the car and placing it in drive.

Unsure of what Marsha meant, Nicole asked. "Did I do okay?"

"Okay?" Marsha laughed. "You blew my fuckin' socks off. I wasn't the client, Manny was."

"Well, Manny sure seemed to like it. He gave us each an extra hundred dollars and he wants to see us again next week. You can't fool a fooler. You liked it too!" Nicole laughed, proud of herself for giving Marsha so much pleasure.

About twenty minutes later they arrived back at Marsha's house, and her kids were just getting home from school. Marsha introduced them to Nicole. It didn't take them long to gravitate to her, and start calling her Aunt Nicole, which was fine with Marsha. After losing their father she sometimes felt helpless, and Nicole seemed to enjoy their company. After helping Marsha get the kids ready for bed they decided it was late enough to call the bar, the Blue Onion.

It was eight o'clock when Nicole placed the call and asked to speak with the manager. She felt comfort in knowing that Marsha was listening in on another line.

"It's your dime," Tony Bedsoe answered. "I'd like to speak with the manager."

"Darlin, I'm the manager, bouncer, and doorman. What can I do for you?"

"I'm looking for work."

"What experience do you have? Can you tend bar, dance, what?"

"I'm a dancer," Nicole replied.

"Well, how about giving me an audition sometime next week around six p.m."

"I'll be there." Nicole said flatly. She hung up the phone and hurried from the bedroom into the kitchen where Marsha was just hanging up the phone.

Marsha had a stunned look on her face. "I can't swear to it, but I think it's the guy that called for Harold."

CHAPTER EIGHT
DIRTY DANCING

The following week on a Wednesday afternoon Marsha and Nicole paid Manny a second visit. This session was just successful as the first. Afterwards, Marsha offered to help prepare Nicole for her audition at the Blue Onion the following morning.

Thursday morning at ten o'clock Nicole pulled into the driveway of Marsha's house. It was another sunshiny day and she looked forward to spending time with her new girlfriend.

She sat in the car for a brief moment, thinking about her new found relationship with Marsha. She readily enjoyed the time the two of them spent together, and her children were able to help fill some of the void she felt from the loss of Charlotte. Despite all this she was even more determined to find her daughter's killer. No matter what, it had to be her first priority. Nicole climbed out of the car, walked to the front door and rang the doorbell.

"Door's open!" Marsha called out from the kitchen.

Nicole turned the door knob and walked in. As she entered the kitchen Marsha got on her case.

"Girl, if you're going to be coming over here, then you're going to have to start making yourself at home. If the front door is unlocked, walk in. If you want something from the refrigerator, help yourself. I have five children to take care of, that's enough."

"Yes, Ma'am." Nicole smiled.

"Do you have something to dance in? You're going to need bikini bottoms or a g-string, and some tassels to cover your nipples. At most bars in the city, the girls dance topless. I'm sure that's not going to be a problem for you. If it were me, I would wear a g-string. The more you show, the better performance you'll give, and the better the tips."

"I don't wear underwear," Nicole replied with a smile. "Have you ever danced?"

"Who hasn't? But that was many years ago, before I married Harold and started popping out kids," Marsha laughed. Marsha left the kitchen, walked to her bedroom, opened a dresser drawer and selected the bottom of a bikini swim suit, deciding that it would match Nicole's Platinum blonde hair perfectly. She returned to the kitchen. "Try this on," she offered.

Marsha walked to the living room and turned on the stereo. When Nicole joined her a couple minutes later, she was wearing only the bikini bottoms.

Marsha laughed. "Are you putting on a show for me," she asked.

Naked above the waist, her nipples already hard with a barely concealed excitement, Nicole giggled. "Why not?"

Marsha smiled and continued teaching, "Never dance flat footed. Dance on your toes. Turn from one side to the other and bend at the knees."

Nicole followed her every step.

"That's it. Now flow... use your hips and roll forward and backwards like this."

Nicole was a fast learner.

"You're doing great. You sure you've never danced before?" Marsha quizzed.

"I'm a natural," Nicole giggled. Then she asked, "Do you have any appointments today?"

"No, and they are rarely as simple or as much fun as yesterday,"

"But, I do get to go with you to see Manny next week, don't I?" Nicole asked, bending a leg and turning.

"He invited us both. I expect you to go!"

"Well, maybe we should get in a little practice?" Nicole suggested with a flirtatious smile.

"Maybe we should," Marsha smiled back at the thought.

* * *

Jerry Everhart called Gus at home, "Word on the street is that it was Missy's body that was found in the harbor. Two little black boys found her in some weeds. Shit! Her face was half eaten by crabs."

"How horrible." Gus cringed, at the thought. "Do you have any idea who did it?"

"No. But I pity the son of a bitch if I do find out!"

"If there's anything that I can do, let me know."

"Thanks!" Jerry replied.

* * *

Nicole pulled up and parked in front of the Blue Onion. The front door was propped open, and she could see a man sitting inside on a stool at the bar and a barmaid washing glasses.

As Nicole entered the dim interior a second girl appeared and began restocking the hard liquor. There were three shelves of fifths of whiskey, rums, and vodkas. The shelves were a maze of varieties and brands.

Nicole walked up to the bar and asked the barmaid if the manager was in.

Tony grinned, his eyes already looking her up and down, taking careful note of her perky breasts and tight little body. "I am the manager. What can I do for you?"

"I have an appointment for six o'clock." Nicole was taking careful note of everything about the manager, thinking that he could be involved in some way with her daughters death. She watched him roll a quarter back and forth through his fingers. She took notice of the crutches beside his bar stool and the cast running the entire length of his left leg, wondering if she would be the one to give him more than a busted leg.

"What do you do, sweetheart?"

"I'm a dancer. Do the girls here dance nude," she asked.

"Topless!" Tony replied, "Is that a problem for you?"

"No, of course not."

"The bar is the stage. Have you danced on top of a counter before?"

"No, I haven't."

"Did you bring something to wear to the audition?"

"Yes, of course."

"The changing room is all the way to the back on the left. Get changed, then I'll put a quarter in the jukebox and you can show me what your working with."

"Okay."

Four minutes later Nicole walked out wearing nothing more than the bikini bottom.

"Whoa…whoa, honey!" Tony threw up his hands in laughter. "Those puppies look nice, but if you don't cover those nipples you'll get us shut down."

With a little smile one of the girls handed her a pair of tassels from behind the bar. She quickly covered her nipples, finally prepared for the audition.

"What kind of music do you like, honey?" Tony asked.

"Something upbeat."

At the far end of the bar there were carpeted stairs that the girls used to get up and down from the bar's counter. Tony selected a song and she danced sensually from one end of the counter to the other. When the music stopped, she went down to sit on a stool next to him.

"If you miss a shift, you're fired!"

"Does that mean I'm hired?" Nicole asked, purposely showing her excitement.

"The girls take turns dancing. Five songs at a time. That's usually fifteen minutes. You can keep your tips. Here's some advice babe, always wear a garter belt so the guys have a place to put a tip. When you're not dancing, hustle the guys into buying drinks. Pay more attention to the sailors, because they spend more money. If a guy buys you a glass of champagne you make two dollars and fifty cents. If he buys a bottle you sit in a booth with him until it's gone. On a bottle you make twenty-five dollars. It's not a requirement, but when a guy buys a bottle of champagne, he is expecting the dancer to do something. What you do in the booth is totally your decision. Some of the girls charge fifty to a hundred bucks for a blow job. It's my job to make sure nobody gets out of line with you. Understand?"

"I think so." Nicole said in pretended shyness.

"Honey, these girls drink like fishes and they never get drunk. Do you know why?"

"No."

"It's very dark inside here at night. The girls carry a Seven-Up bottle around with them. They take a drink of champagne, then spit it into the Seven-Up bottle. When the bottle gets suspiciously full, they ask the bartender to exchange it for another one. He empties the bottle, goes through the motion of twisting the cap off a new bottle and hands it right back to them. Now empty."

Nicole laughed.

Tony smiled, rolled the quarter slowly between his fingers, flipped it into the air, then caught it.

"When do I start?"

"You already have. You're working until two in the morning. The other girls start at eight. Until then, if a guy comes in and puts a quarter in the jukebox you get your ass up on the counter and shake your ass."

"What's your stage name?"

"Peaches," Nicole replied. It was the first name that came to her mind. She was born in Georgia, so it seemed appropriate. Names were unimportant in the bar. There were no taxes taken out and the girls were paid at the end of every night.

"Do I have time to run out and buy a garter belt?"

Tony chuckled. "Sure, go ahead. Don't ever park in front of the club. Be smart. You don't want anyone knowing your car or tag number."

As the girls arrived for work she introduced herself as 'Peaches'.

That night she met Stormy, Amber, Sassy, and Jolene. Nicole drank some of the champagne because she needed the liquid courage.

When it was her turn to dance she mimicked some of the other girls' moves, adding a few of her own. She kept her purse under the bar filling it with tips when she walked off the stage. The patrons were loud, boisterous, and obnoxious. But despite all this, they empowered her. Throughout the night they yelled for Peaches. One right after another, they bought her glasses of champagne. Two sailors bought bottles. For twenty five dollars she gave one a hand job, feeling no emotions about what she was willing to do or how far she was willing to go. For fifty, she never hesitated when it came time for her to give a sailor a blow job. When she finished for the night, she had three hundred and thirty dollars, including tips.

Three days later Nicole decided that it was time to move to a new residence. The small efficiency apartment was closing in on her. She needed more space. She needed a place she could feel comfortable coming home to. Looking through the Classifieds of the Baltimore Sun, she found an apartment outside of the city, but closer to the Blue Onion. After a quick walk through, she rented it. Then, she went shopping. She bought a new color television at an appliance store. At a Women's Apparel store she purchased several string bikinis and some nipple tassels.

Her last stop was at AT&T to have a phone installed in her new apartment.

Returning to her new home, she looked in her purse in search of whatever cocaine she had left. It was almost time to pay Charlie another visit, she was almost out of product. She laid out her usual double lines and snorted one up each nostril.

Nicole wondered what Dave was doing? Did he ever think of her? She chuckled at the thought because she damn sure hadn't given him a second thought until now. She wondered how long he had worked for the Anne Arundel County Sheriff's Department? As a detective, he certainly wasn't the sharpest tack in the box. How could he have overlooked something so simple as asking Marsha if she thought she could make a voice identification? How could a seasoned investigator miss that? She hadn't! Now, she was following up on her own, fully prepared to do whatever it took to find her daughter's murderer. Thoughts of Charlotte, and remembering the sight of her being crushed by the speeding car, brought tears to her eyes. She held herself partially responsible. The guilt she felt for allowing her baby to play in the street was almost more than she could bear. Things like this weren't supposed to happen in suburban neighborhoods on a quiet street, especially where groups of children were known for playing in the street. Despite knowing this, she could not escape from her own sense of blame.

CHAPTER NINE

TOUGH KITTY

Nicole once again drove unannounced over to Charlie's house and pounded on the door. This time when Charlie opened the door he wore a big smile.

"Damn," he said. "I saw you through the peephole. What did you do to yourself? You look hot."

"You like my hair," she teased, fluffing her hair. "I came to get the rest of my things."

"You really do look good," he licked his lips, eyeing her pointy breasts.

"Thanks Charlie, but I didn't come to hear your lame ass compliments," she frowned at him. "And while we're at it, I need another eighth."

"It's going to cost you!" Charlie's smile suddenly brightened.

"I've got money," she replied, opening her purse.

"I don't want your money," he grinned.

Nicole laughed knowingly, but wanted to hear him say it. "Tell me what you want."

"Here's the deal. I'll give you the best cocaine you've ever had, but you have to give me a blow job and some pussy."

"Give me the stuff first!"

Charlie lived up to his part of the bargain and Nicole gave him the best suck and fuck of his life.

"We never... had sex like... that before." Charlie huffed. He was physically spent.

"You never paid for it before. Don't get it twisted Charlie. It was just sex and you got what you paid for!"

* * *

"Sorry, Detective Marks. My informant wants to remain anonymous. His wearing a wire is out of the question. He's not willing to cooperate any further."

"Well, I don't think it will serve any purpose to talk to the Ever-hart's. They've been around the block more that once, so they would simply lawyer up. Let's wait and hopefully something else pops up."

"My informant is obviously concerned for his well being and that tells me he fears Dick and Jerry Everhart."

* * *

Detective Daniels of the Baltimore County Sheriffs Department traced the last call made to the Bennett's residence to a phone at the Blue Onion. Nicole was busy dancing on the bar when he dropped in and asked to speak to the manager. She observed the detective show Tony his badge and watched out of the corner of her eyes as the two men disappeared into the back office.

Fifteen minutes later, the detective left. Tony stood at the front entrance to the bar rolling a quarter through his fingers, flipping it in the air, then catching it. Nicole noted that he did not appear to be disturbed or worried. The detective, on the other hand appeared to be upset. He had hurried from the bar without even a glance at the nearly nude girls. She wondered if it was just some cop Tony had to pay off to keep the heat off of the club. At the moment she had no way of knowing what was true or false. There were still a lot of unanswered questions.

Nicole finished her time on the counter top and was coming from behind the bar to circulate amongst the many male customers when she was bumped hard by the dancer known as 'Stormy.'

"The new girl always does better than the other girls. You're noth-ing but fresh meat!" Stormy laughed in her face.

"You're just jealous!" Nicole replied coldly.

"Honey, you ain't got nothing to be jealous of." Stormy cupped her hands and proudly displayed her firm rack of thirty eight double-D's.

Nicole knew her tits were small, but they were firm and good enough for her. "Anything more than a mouthful is a waste," she sneered, firing back.

Without any further provocation Stormy slapped Nicole. The beast living within Nicole reared its ugly head. Without a second thought, or a moments hesitation, Nicole grabbed Stormy by her hair with her left hand and slugged her repeatedly with her right. Nicole's eyes were fiery red as she relentlessly pounded on Stormy's head. Drunken sailors and customers alike, cheered the girls on. Tony heard the excitement from his place at the front door of the club. He could hear the customers rooting, "Peaches! Peaches! Peaches!" as he ran towards the girls to break up the fight.

"Mutha fucker!" Tony cursed, grabbing Nicole around the waist and picking her up, her little feet kicking in the air. She had a solid grip on Stormy's hair. "Let the bitch go," he ordered. Nicole immediately released her hair. Tony stood between them. "What the fuck just happened here," he demanded, his face twisted in outrage.

Stormy's face was already swelling with bruising. Nicole had no more than a slight blush from where Stormy had slapped her. The victory was clearly Nicole's. No one could dispute that.

"The both of you, in my office now!"

Tony sat behind a desk with both girls in front of him. They were breathing hard, but ready for round two.

"This is a business. We are all here to make money, right? If you want to fight take up boxing or mud wrestling. If there's anymore fighting, you're both fired. Do we understand each other? Now, you two kiss and make up."

"I'm sorry, Peaches," Stormy offered, suddenly smiling and giggling.

"Me too!" Nicole smiled.

* * *

"This is Detective Daniel's from the Homicide Division of the Baltimore County Sheriffs Department. Is this Detective Hill?"

"Yes, it is. What can I do for you?"

"I'm investigating a homicide. Last night I interviewed the manager of a bar called the Blue Onion. The manager, Tony Bedsoe, informed me that you had already interviewed him?"

"That's correct."

"If you interfere in my investigation again I will report you to my supervisor."

"Your investigation? I'm investigating an assault that has now been labeled a murder. The assailant escaped in a stolen car. While making good his getaway he ran over a six year old girl, killing her instantly. I traced calls made to the Bennett residence from the pay phone at the Blue Onion. Marsha Bennett is a Call girl and you're investigating the murder of her husband, Harold. I think that makes this investigation just as much mine as it does yours."

"I wasn't aware of that," Detective Daniels admitted.

"Well, now you know!" Sergeant Hill snapped, then slammed down the phone.

* * *

Throughout the night, Stormy and Peaches laughed, joked, and bonded. When the bar closed Stormy asked Nicole if she had ever been to 'The Block', which was just another name for Baltimore Street. A city street lined with strip clubs, peep shows, and adult book stores. "That's where the big bucks are. But it's next to impossible to get a job at any of those clubs. The clubs are closed by now, but the peep shows are open all night."

"Let's go!" Peaches smiled.

Stormy put the top down on her yellow Pontiac convertible and the girls cruised the strip known as 'The Block.' Stormy stopped at a peep show. It also sold nudity magazines and adult toys. Stormy watched in surprise as Nicole bought an assortment of toys. The neon lights were colorful and drunken sailors stumbled down the sidewalk trying to make their way back to their ships. A couple of prostitutes leaned against a building smoking cigarettes and blowing smoke rings in the air.

"Would you like to visit the Wee Hours?" Stormy asked.

"What's that?"

"It's an after hours club. I know the owner, Gus. It's not far from here."

"Let's go."

When they arrived at the after hour club Stormy introduced Nicole to Gus as 'Peaches' and he immediately told her his rules. "If you take a trick out of my club you owe me fifteen bucks in advance. Don't bring any drugs into my club, and if I catch you using or in possession of any drugs, you will be barred from coming here."

"I bet you say that to all the girls." Peaches replied smiling.

"I do." Gus grinned.

Nicole was quickly making her way into the underground world of pimps, prostitutes and drug dealers. She was determined to find the man responsible for killing her daughter.

* * *

Marsha was baking cookies when Nicole walked into the kitchen. "Well, aren't you quite the Susie homemaker!"

"I'm every man's dream. Betty Crocker in the kitchen, and Xavier Hollander in the bedroom. Where have you been? I've been worried sick about you."

"Working." Nicole announced. proud of herself. "Would you like to know my stage name?"

"What is it?" Marsha asked, stopping what she doing to listen.

"Peaches!" Nicole blurted out. "And I got into a fight with one of the other dancers."

"A fight?" Marsha raised a questioning eyebrow.

"I kicked ass!" Nicole snickered. "The girl that I got into a fight with name is Stormy. We're cool now. She took me to a peep show on Baltimore Street. Baltimore Street is called 'The Block'. Afterwards, we went to an after-hour club called the Wee Hours."

"Nothing with you surprises me anymore."

"Yes, it will." Nicole laughed.

"What's that supposed to mean?" Marsha asked, smiling.

"Just that I'm full of surprises. Did you make those cookies fresh?"

"Fresh out of the box." Marsha laughed. "The kids love them. We're going to be late getting to our appointment with Manny. I've already called to let him know."

"Why are we going to be late?"

"My babysitter. As soon as she gets here we will leave. I don't want the kids coming home from school to an empty house."

"That's cool." Nicole understood, and she respected Marsha for putting her kids first.

When the phone rang Nicole answered it, "Hello?"

"May I speak to Marsha Bennett?" came the male voice.

"It's for you," she passed the wall receiver to her.

"Hello?"

"Marsha Bennett?"

"Yes, it is."

"This is Detective Daniels from the Baltimore County Sheriffs Department. We spoke once, but I need to ask you a few more questions. Detective Sergeant Hill from the Anne Arundel County Sheriffs Department informed me that you are a Call girl?"

"That son of a bitch!" Marsha shouted. "If I am, it has nothing to do with my husband's murder. If you have any more questions, talk to my attorney!" Marsha snapped, slamming down the receiver.

"What was that all about?" Nicole asked.

"That fucking Sergeant Hill. He told me that he was going to be discreet. Instead, he's telling everyone about my personal life. He told you, and now he's told a Baltimore County detective I'm a Call girl. That shit pisses me off!"

* * *

Manny was happy to see the girls. He was already dressed in his white robe and their money was counted and neatly placed on the dining room table. Six crisp one hundred dollar bills.

"Would you girls like a drink," he offered.

"Do you like surprises?" Nicole asked Manny, swinging a large brown purse back and forth in her right hand.

"That depends on what the surprise is," he grinned.

Deciding not to have a drink, Marsha and Nicole walked into the bedroom, undressed each other, and laid down on the round bed. The satin sheets cool to the touch. Nicole kissed Marsha and played with her pussy until it was nice and wet.

Then she reached inside her purse, pulled out a large vibrator and slowly inserted it into Marsha's wet pussy twisting the handle turning it to vibrate at the highest of its three settings. Marsha gasped in surprised pleasure.

"Toys, Manny. That's the surprise. How do you feel about toys," she giggled.

"Absolutely wonderful!" Manny stood over the bed the front of his robe already tenting up with his excitement. He was breathing hard and grinning from ear to ear.

"You... are... full... of surprises," Marsha gasped.

Nicole sucked on Marsha's nipples, inserting the silver rocket deeper into her friend's pussy. She pulled it out and massaged her clit lowering the speed of the vibrator. At the precise moment that Marsha's body arched Nicole turned the vibrator back up to its highest setting and worked it feverishly in and out of her wanting pussy. Marsha bucked wildly, moaned, and arched her back in the throes of sheer ecstasy. Nicole looked to see if Manny was enjoying her performance. He had moved to sit in his favorite chair and was sporting a healthy hard-on. Nicole got up from the bed, seductively walked over and stood before Manny, then dropped to her knees and quickly put his manhood into her mouth. Marsha mounted Nicole from behind and shoved the silver rocket deep into her ass while fingering her moist pussy with her other hand. As Marsha brought Nicole to a shattering orgasm, Nicole swallowed Manny's cum and sucked him dry. It had been a very long time since Manny had felt the sensation of having an orgasm. His eyes filled with tears of gratitude and he gave the girls an extra two hundred dollars each.

"What kind of work do you do?" Nicole asked Manny as she dressed.

"I'm retired," he replied, then elaborated. "I am the retired owner of Bethlehem Steel."

"Bethlehem Steel. As in Sparrow's Point." Nicole said in surprise. Nicole recalled that both Jeff Miles and Harold Bennett had been employed there. She surmised Manny to be super rich. "I'll make you a deal, Manny. You continue to pay Marsha and I will come here every week with her if you will buy me a car."

"Are you sure you want to make that deal," he asked. He had just given her five hundred dollars. At three hundred dollars a week it amounted to twelve hundred a month. Nicole could buy herself several new cars. One new car was a bargain for him. Besides, Manny liked the idea of locking in the weekly visits.

"What do you say?" Nicole smiled sweetly.

Manny laughed, admitting to himself that he was totally captivated by the little blonde. "Pick out whatever you want."

"I want a brand new silver Mercedes Benz."

"Pick it out and have the salesman call me."

Wasting no time that afternoon, Nicole picked out a silver Mercedes convertible. It came with a gray leather interior and it was fully loaded.

Marsha would have never made that deal. She was more business savvy than Nicole. But thanks to Nicole, she now had weekly payments she could now count on. Manny paid for the car. He purchased a lifetime warranty and title fees, taxes, and for the license plate. When Nicole picked up the Mercedes Benz, she was given a clear title, letting her know that the vehicle was paid for in full.

CHAPTER TEN

TROUBLE IN PARADISE

Over the years Nicole had grown attached to her little yellow Volkswagen. Around town and to work she mostly drove the Bug, but on Wednesday's when she went to see Marsha and Manny she usually drove the Mercedes. And for her new Mercedes Nicole paid extra to special order a personalized license plate with her stage name 'Peaches' engraved on it. She could hardly wait to see the expression on Charlie's face when she showed off her new car.

Two weeks later, Nicole moved to a nicer apartment in a high-rise building known as Regency Towers. She purchased all new furnishings, a King sized bed, and enough new clothes to fill up the large walk-in closet. The apartment offered underground parking for a monthly fee. Nicole paid for two parking spaces. She installed an alarm on the Mercedes and purchased a protective cover for the new Benz.

Even though it was not a part of her plan, Nicole discovered that she enjoyed living the fast life. She was enjoying every minute of the attention from the men. And she loved even more the money they stuffed in her garter belt. It was mostly dollar bills, but every now and then she would find a five, ten, or twenty at the end of the night. For her, it was like having a big fan club and she loved it.

Manny reminded her a lot of her dad and she wondered if her dad was alive if he would have been a dirty old man too. She hoped he would. She hoped he would have been able to enjoy life just as much as Manny. Nicole adored Manny, and it was not about the money. Admittedly, it helped. But she felt something much more special for Manny, much like she felt for Marsha. They were like a dirty little family with secrets that were kept locked behind closed doors. She always looked forward to their Wednesday afternoons together.

* * *

The Blue Onion was 'poppin' ... as Peaches liked to call it. The front door was once again propped open due to the ungodly heat. The club was filled well over capacity but as long as he never got caught Tony cared nothing about the number of customers inside the building. The fire Inspector normally came around once a month during the daytime hours to check the fire extinguishers to make sure they were updated and in good working condition, then he checked the exit doors to make sure they were not deadlocked. State law required that, in case of a fire, there be more than one exit out of the building. Tonight the bar was filled with cigarette smoke and as Nicole danced she watched tendrils of smoke drifting out of the open front door. Before that moment she had paid no attention to the man Tony was talking to near the door. Now she noticed that the man never smiled or made any attempt to show a friendliness towards Tony. Whatever they were talking about went unheard over the noise of the bar, and soon Tony and the mystery man walked towards the back office.

"Problem? There's no problem," Tony was saying as he closed the office door. "I took care of that guy. The cops traced a call to the public pay phone here. Anyone could have made that call, right? Two cops came in asking if I knew some guy named Ralph. He's the guy that supposedly made the call."

"Is there a problem?" Domonic asked a second time.

"No, I iced the creep! I did it myself and there's no witnesses. He wanted his money back, so I figured the best thing to do was to get rid of the problem. Did you know you ran over a six year old girl? You crushed the kid like a grape and she died instantly. Miles is dead too. Let me tell you, the cops are real pissed off over that little girl being killed."

"You iced the guy yourself?" Crowbar asked doubtfully.

"Yeah! I took him out to Baltimore County and put six slugs in him. Two of them right between the eyes," Tony bragged.

"Don't be trying to take my job," Crowbar replied, his poor attempt at a joke.

Tony took him seriously. "I wouldn't try to do that," he protested. "I was afraid the smuck would talk."

"So was I!" Domonic admitted.

Tony and Domonic talked for another few minutes, then left the office and seated themselves at the crowded bar.

"Give Domonic whatever he wants to drink. Make it on the house."

"Who's the new girl?" Domonic asked, staring up between Nicole's legs as she danced.

"She's Peaches. A real class act that one. Spunky little shit too. Within her first few nights here she whipped Stormy's ass," Tony chuckled.

Nicole looked at Crowbar and smiled, rolling her hips slowly at him. He motioned for her to come closer. When she did, he stuffed a twenty dollar bill into her garter belt.

"Thank you!" Nicole said smiling.

Domonic finished his drink, and left. He never felt comfortable being in a crowd unless he had his back to a wall, and that was not possible unless he sat in a corner booth with a view of the entire room.

As Nicole exited the stage Stormy signaled for her.

"Stay away from that one," she warned Peaches. "He's bad news!" That was probably more than she should have said, but she was hoping Peaches would hear her. Nicole had a mind of her own and she would do exactly what it is she wanted to do. As if she had not already proven that to everyone. There was something about Domonic that made him stand out from the other guys. She was unsure what that was, but she knew there was definitely a serious connection between Tony and Domonic.

* * *

One of the things Marsha had told Nicole was that she never took her shoes off for less than a hundred dollars. Nicole thought it was a good rule to live by, and it would be hers, too. When the bar closed she sat down in a booth to count her money. It was her best night ever, over four hundred dollars. Suddenly she decided she wanted to celebrate her successful night.

Nicole left the bar and drove the Bug to Regency Towers. She parked the Bug in the underground garage next to her covered Mercedes Benz, then took the elevator up to her apartment. She showered, dressed in tight fitting blue jeans and a plain white T-shirt, then hurriedly went back downstairs to the underground garage, uncovered the Mercedes, put the top down, and cruised over to Charlie's apartment taking in the peacefulness of the quite night. When she pulled into the parking lot she was surprised to see the lights were on in his apartment in the early morning hour. Standing outside the driver's door, Charlie was half drunk, coked out, and Nicole was a feast for his eyes. He hurried down the steps.

"This car isn't really yours," he questioned her doubtfully.

"It's mine!" Nicole snickered.

"Where did you get the money to buy something like this? Did you have an insurance policy for Charlotte?"

"Fuck you, Charlie," she cursed him. "That's a terrible thing for you to say. I don't know how you could even bring yourself to think of something like that? I had no insurance policy!"

"I'm sorry," Charlie apologized. Nicole had never known Charlie to apologize for anything he said or did, so his apology was well received.

"The title and registration are in the glove compartment. The title is free and clear," she smiled proudly.

"How did you manage this?" Charlie marveled.

"That's none of your business, Charlie," she laughed.

"Wanna get lucky?" Charlie grinned.

"Have you got an eighth?"

"Damn it, Nicole. Don't do me like that!"

"Excuse me, I seem to recall you throwing me out of your apartment, and saying the pussy's good, but not that good. I had no money,

Charlie. So if you want some of my pussy, it's going to cost you."

"You fucking bitch," Charlie said with a grin.

Nicole giggled and Charlie gave her the eighth of cocaine in advance. She had always been attractive, but with her platinum blonde hair she was stunningly beautiful, especially naked.

* * *

"Hello, Marsha?"

"Yes."

"This is Sergeant Hill. I just called to check on you. How are you doing?"

"How do you think I'm doing? My husband is dead and you're running around telling everyone that I'm a fuckin' whore."

"I never told anyone that!"

"Is that right? First, some girl beats on my front door shouting, 'You're going to talk to me, bitch!' When I do, she tells me that you told her I was a Call girl."

"Nicole Redman? When did you see her?"

Without answering his question, Marsha continued. "Then I got a call from a Detective Daniels from the Baltimore County Sheriffs Department and he informs me that you told him I was a Call girl and now he wants to interview me a second time…"

"Marsha, do you know where I can find Nicole?"

"I don't think she's interested in seeing you. She told me that you've got a little dick and you're horrible in the sack." Marsha hung up the phone. There was some satisfaction in mentioning that his penis was small, even though Nicole had said no such thing.

Sergeant Hill dialed Charlie's number.

"Hello?" Charlie answered.

"Charlie, Sergeant Hill. Have you seen Nicole lately?"

"Yeah! I fucked her last night. She's got platinum blonde hair and she's driving a new Mercedes Benz," Charlie chuckled and hung up the phone.

"Asshole!" Sergeant Hill said aloud. He did not believe a word that Charlie said. He wondered what in the world Nicole was up to?

CHAPTER ELEVEN

FLORIDA SNOW

Charlie flew into Naples Florida, rented a car, and drove to Marco Island where his friend Brad "Juice" Bernhagen lived in a two bedroom condo overlooking the ocean. It was a gorgeous day. The sky was a clear cloudless blue and the gulf's water crystal clear. The sand was as white as sugar and hot on bare feet. Two dolphins playfully swam within fifty feet of the shoreline and scores of women wearing string bikinis laid on towels, played volleyball, and roamed up and down the beach. But Charlie was not there to chase the many young girls, he was there to work. Late one evening, with no more than a half an hours notice, he would hop into a speedboat with Juice and they would speed out to sea to meet a fishing boat, a freighter, or a cargo ship to pick-up their cargo of illegal cocaine. The transfer was always made twelve miles out to sea in international waters. The United States had no jurisdiction beyond the twelve-mile limit, and fishing boats were easiest to unload. If it was a freighter, or cargo ship, someone would throw packages into the water and it was Charlie's job to locate and haul the packages on board. Even with two flashlights tied to each package, as they bobbed up and down in the open water they were sometimes hard to find. Charlie dreaded the thought of an airplane flying overhead, or a passing boat, seeing the lighted packages.

After loading the powerboat they raced across the water in total darkness. Juice never chanced someone seeing their running lights. It was just blind luck they never hit something. That was Charlie's greatest fear.

The Donzi speedboat was built for racing, having been equipped with twin 327 high performance engines. On a normal run they hauled two hundred kilos of cocaine. Once a month Charlie flew to Naples, rented a car and helped Juice make the run. Juice never complained, so Charlie never complained. After each successful trip they partied hard, hitting all of the night spots.

Charlie and Juice's history went back to their time in prison. They served two years together at The Maryland House of Corrections, more commonly referred to as 'Jessup's Cut.' The prison's nickname was derived from two things. 'Jessup's' because the prison was in Jessup, Maryland. 'Cut' due to the daily stabbings. Stabbings became so routine the emergency siren never sounded. The siren became reserved for riot conditions only. Brad and Charlie shared a cell, the upper bunk having become Charlie's living space a week before Brad's arrival. It wasn't long until Brad was telling Charlie stories about his growing up in Florida. Stories that Charlie found fascinating, but hard to believe. One of the things that Charlie doubted most of all, was that Juice had ever seen a ton of cocaine.

To support himself in prison, Brad made hooch. Homemade wine. It was given different names. 'Plum Crazy' was made some plumbs. 'Apple Jack' was made from apples. 'Sunshine' was made from oranges. The most popular and most potent was 'Mash'. It was made from potatoes and its nickname was coined by men serving in the United States Army. It was the simple tale of how Brad Bernhagen had come into the nickname of 'Juice'. When Juice was released from prison, he sent Charlie photos of girls in bikinis and a One Hundred dollar Money Order every month. Juice was sure of one thing. No matter what, Charlie always had his back.

Two days after Charlie was released, he received a package in the mail with a Florida return address. Charlie peeled off the brown wrapping only to discover there was another layer of brown wrapping. One after another, he peeled off four layers with foot powder sprinkled between the last two layers. The bottom layer was sealed with gray duck tape. At the sight of what was in the final package, Charlie smiled. It was a kilo of cocaine mailed from a bogus address with a note telling him to get on his feet. Charlie did just that. His first major purchase was a 1965 blue Corvette Stingray.

Now, one year later, it was a beautiful night and they were sitting in the Donzi twelve miles out to sea waiting for a shrimp boat. The sky was clear, the air warm, and the waves gently rocked the boat.

Charlie was elated that it was not a freighter, or a cargo ship, this time. When Juice saw the lights of an approaching boat he signaled by turning a flashlight on and off three times.

As the shrimp boat neared the Donzi, out of curiosity, Charlie asked Juice where he bought the Donzi.

"I have a friend who makes high performance boats in Miami, Don Aranow. He owns Apache Performance Boats. The Donzi was a trade-in. He's sold two boats to the D.E.A."

"That's nice to hear," Charlie said sarcastically.

Juice chuckled. "The heat is generally on the other coast, around Miami. That's where the big boys play. We're just little fish in a great big ocean," Juice chuckled. Juice was six-one, a solid two hundred pounds. He was born and raised in Florida, but his parents immigrated from Sweden. He had blonde hair, blue eyes, and a well tanned and well toned body. Charlie often thought with Juice's chiseled six-pack, he looked like a Greek statue. The only six-pack Charlie ever had was six cans of Budweiser. No one could ever mistake them as brothers. Comparing Charlie to Juice was like comparing apples to oranges.

It took less than thirty minutes to load the speedboat. They gave a parting wave to the men on the shrimp boat and raced off into the night, cruising at speeds of sixty miles an hour without running lights. Juice and Charlie stood at the helm peering over the windshield searching the dark water for any floating objects. Their eyes watered as the Donzi lunged forward, jumping from the top of one wave to another. When Juice saw the lights of houses near the shoreline, he slowed to forty miles per hour and turned the running lights on. The idea was not to bring any unnecessary attention to themselves.

Ten minutes later, they docked at a private residence where a white van and two men anxiously waited their arrival. The foursome quickly unloaded the kilos and carried them to the van. There was no greeting, conversation, or exchange of good tidings. A week later, Charlie would receive a package in the mail containing a kilo of cocaine for his one nights work.

Daylight was peeping over the horizon as Charlie untied the ropes securing the Donzi to the dock. As he shoved the boat away from the pier Juice started the engines and put the boat in reverse, slowly backing up. Clear of the dock, he switched to the forward gear and steadily increased speed. Then, he glanced at Charlie and announced. "You need a nickname. Nobody in this business uses their real name. So, I'm going to give you one. How about 'Spoon' or 'Spooner'. No, I've got it. 'Peanut'. It fits you. You're head is shaped like a peanut, so your nickname is now 'Peanut'.

"Why can't I be named after a super hero, like Hercules."

"Because it doesn't fit you, Peanut." Juice grinned.

"What's on the agenda for tonight?" Charlie asked, anxious to party.

"Sleep! We're getting up early to drive to Miami. From there we're flying to an island in the Bahamas."

* * *

The following morning, they drove to Miami International Airport and boarded a twin engine turbo prop airplane. When they were airborne, Juice told Charlie they were flying to an unspoiled island called, Great Exuma.

"From now on," Juice explained, "I will call you Peanut. No one needs to know your real name. Do you know what dry snitching is?"

"Of course. It's when I tell someone your business, and you end up busted. Ultimately, it's my fault."

"Exactly! I know a guy that dry snitched. He was wrapped in chicken wire, weighted down with cinder blocks tied to his feet, and shoved off the back of a boat into the ocean as he screamed and pleaded for his life. The sad thing is, he was a solid guy. He just ran his mouth too much."

"That's a horrible way to meet your maker," Charlie reflected.

As the airplane flew over small uninhabited islands, looking from his window Charlie saw sunken boats and airplanes. On one small island, he saw a landing strip carved into the woods with fifty gallon oil drums lining both sides. It was obvious what it was used for.

Forty-five minutes after take-off, the airplane landed on a dirt runway on the island of Great Exuma. At the far end of the runway there was an old rusty yellow John-Deere bulldozer. Charlie wondered if it was still in use. Customs was a small unpainted concrete building. Once inside, there was a long wooden table for the passengers to place their luggage on for inspection. Two black Bahamian men dressed in dark green Bermuda shorts with matching shirts searched through the luggage and asked several routine questions.

It was in one door, and out the other, to pass through Customs and only was a short walk to a grass shack across the street. A wooden plaque hung above the entrance door that simply read 'Kermits'. As they walked into the bar Charlie took note of his surroundings. A thin black man, conservatively dressed, was seated at the bar talking with the bartender who was also a Bahamian. The two men turned their attention to Juice.

With a huge grin, the man seated at the bar stood welcoming Juice with a quick embrace and a slap on the back. "It's good to see you, my friend."

From behind the bar the owner, Kermit, asked. "What's your pleasure? The drinks are on the house." It was obvious the men had enjoyed a long standing relationship.

Juice introduced Charlie, ordered two drinks, and the men talked catching up on old times. Vernon offered them a place to stay. Juice respectfully declined, explaining they had reservations at the Peace and Plenty, his favorite motel.

As they talked, Charlie learned there were only two motels and three bars on the small island. And, no paved roads. The Bahamians were black, but spoke with a thick British accent.

Kermit said that Lord Rholes deeded sixty percent of the island to the Bahamians, that it was generation land and could never be sold.

Vernon Curtis was Kermit's partner and Governor Pinling's nephew. Their partnership included a boat that picked up and delivered the mail to and from Miami.

Vernon offered to give Juice and Charlie a ride into Georgetown. Since there were no taxi's, Juice accepted his offer without a moment's hesitation. Vernon steered the old white Dodge windowed van right and left dodging pot holes in the unkept dirt road. Georgetown was less than a block long and shaped like a horseshoe with an assortment of stores and a wooden planked sidewalk. In the middle, there was a courtyard. At the far end, a two story concrete building was painted pink. That was City Hall. Charlie wondered what qualified it as a town.

Juice thanked Vernon for the ride and told Charlie that it was only a short walk to the harbor; explaining that he had rented a boat.

"Where are we going?" Charlie asked.

"We are going to visit a friend who owns an island not very far from here."

The boat ride was much rougher than Juice had expected, but it was daylight and there was very little risk of their capsizing. Arriving at their destination, Charlie removed his shoes, rolled his pant legs up, jumped out of the boat, and pulled it to shore. They were met by three heavily armed men wearing shorts and tank tops.

Juice yelled out. "John Leder invited us!"

The men quickly surrounded them. At gun point, they were escorted into the tress. After trekking through the woods for a short distance, they were led to a small bungalow.

"Welcome my friend. This must be, Charlie." John Leder grinned from his place on the front porch. Leder was medium height, average weight, with dark hair and brown eyes. He looked as though he hadn't shaven in days. His dark skin was either Mexican, Columbian, or Cuban. Charlie's guess was Columbian. He shook the hand John Leder offered him.

The island was known as Norman's Cay. Many people had lost

their lives for getting too close to the island, or for being too nosy.

"I thought my name was Peanut?" Charlie whispered to Juice.

"I just gave you that name yesterday. Last week you were Charlie," Juice laughed.

"I have a business proposition for you, Charlie. Juice vouches for you. He says that you are trustworthy and I'm looking to expand my business to the East Coast. I will provide you with as many kilos of cocaine as you can sell for eighteen thousand a kilo, delivered wherever you want. You can resell them for twenty-eight thousand. Forty in New York!"

"I have no money to pay for the kilos, and I've never sold any quanity," Charlie spoke earnestly.

"We all start out small, Charlie. Do you think that I started out big? I will front you whatever you want. But always have my money, or my cocaine."

"Start me with ten kilos," Charlie offered.

"I will send no less than fifty."

"Can I return those if things don't work out?"

"Absolutely, Charlie. But don't think negative. I believe you will do very well."

The deal was sealed with a handshake.

Then, John extended his hospitality offering lines of cocaine and a parting gift in a plastic baggy. They returned to Great Exuma.

* * *

To Charlie's dismay, there was no television or phone in their motel room. Windowed double doors opened to the balcony where waves splashed against a retaining wall below. Sailboats were moored in the small cove. Later that evening, when they went to the motel's restaurant, Charlie learned the Bahamians had three speeds which they lived by. Slow, slower, and slowest. After dinner they moved to the bar where he ordered a drink favored by tourists. It was called a

'Goombay Smash'. Made from a concoction of rums, it was extremely sweet. One drink knocked Charlie for a loop, and he retired to his room early. He awoke the following morning to the sound of waves splashing against the retaining wall, and with a throbbing headache. Charlie slowly climbed out of bed. He took four aspirin, showered, shaved, and dressed.

On the flight back to Miami, Charlie thanked Juice for vouching for him. "With this new responsibility, I may not be able to help you every month," he added.

"You have already been replaced." Juice said, with a grin.

"How did you know that I would accept the offer?"

"Only a fool would have turned it down," Juice laughed.

"Let's celebrate! Tonight Let's hit all the clubs in Miami and party until we drop." Charlie suggested.

In Charlie's opinion, no city could be compared to Miami. Not even the great city of Las Vegas. Miami had gorgeous babes in every shape, size, and color. It was a melting pot of nationalities, and the girls were all hot and looking for three things. Drugs, sex, and money.

Charlie and Juice spent the day shopping before renting a room at the Holiday Inn on Mango Drive. After dressing in the most expensive suits their money could buy, Juice held out two boxes in his right hand and told Charlie to pick one. Inside the boxes were identical 14k gold chains with matching medallions made from Pike's Peak gold.

"I don't know what to say." Charlie grinned, admiring his gift.

"No one else has these. We are brothers, Charlie. Always remember, I've got your back!"

"Likewise!" Charlie swore his allegiance.

With the chains around their necks, they stood next to each other admiring themselves in the mirror.

Juice pulled the parting gift from John Leder from his pocket, laid out four lines of cocaine, rolled up a dollar bill, and passed it to Charlie. "You first!"

After snorting their lines, they left the motel and drove down

Ocean Drive. Juice drew in a deep breath of the ocean's air, and said. "You have winters, Charlie. But Florida has the real snow!"

"Florida snow. Cocaine!" Charlie laughed heartily.

CHAPTER TWELVE

MONKEY BUSINESS

After a long night at the Blue Onion an exhausted Nicole drove straight home and went right to bed, the sheets were cool to the touch and inviting. Wednesday morning she awoke to the buzzing of the alarm clock. She reached for the night stand beside the bed to turn it off, noticing the time was nine o'clock. As her eyes focused, the sun shined brightly through the bedroom window. Thoughts of seeing Marsha and Manny later that afternoon was enough to motivate her. Nicole yawned, slowly crawled out of bed, walked to the bathroom, and showered. She shaved her legs, then spent another fifteen minutes blow drying her hair. She walked barefoot to her bedroom closet and selected a pair of white Levi's, a yellow halter top, and slid her tiny feet into a pair of flip flops.

Nicole's next stop was the kitchen. For breakfast, she buttered two slices of toast and drank a glass of orange juice. After breakfast, she washed dishes and cleaned the apartment, using the cleaning to relax her mind.

At one o'clock Nicole left the apartment taking the elevator to the underground garage. "It's not your day," she said to the Bug as she removed the protective cover from the Mercedes. She drove to Marsha's house, parked in the driveway, opened the front door and walking inside, unannounced. Nicole heard the unmistakable sound of frying grease. She sniffed the air, and tried to guess what Marsha was cooking. Fried chicken, she guessed. She tip toed into the kitchen, grabbed Marsha by the waist, and shouted. "Boo!"

"Nice try," Marsha giggled. "I heard you come through, the front door."

"What have you found out?"

"I'm not sure. Tony was talking to a guy who gave me a twenty dollar tip. His name is Domonic. I can't explain it, but I have a real funny feeling about him."

One pot and a skillet sat atop red coils on the stove as Marsha prepared dinner. She stopped to look at Nicole. "Always go with your instincts! That's what God gave them to you for." Marsha turned a burner off.

"What happened to you?" Nicole demanded, staring at the make-up covering a bruise on Marsha's face."

"I told you, not everyone is as nice as Manny. I have a client that gets off pretending he's raping a woman. He got a little carried away, but he pays well. He gave me six hundred dollars."

There's not enough money in the world to allow someone to mistreat you!" Nicole declared in anger. "Do you want me to beat the asshole up for you?"

"No!" Marsha laughed, grateful for her concern. Marsha turned the pork chops in the frying pan, then turned off the burner. "Dinner is cooked," she announced, proud of her motherly duties. Without further small talk, they grabbed their purses and walked out of the house.

"It's a beautiful day, isn't it?" Marsha smiled.

"Let's take my car." Nicole offered, not answering Marsha' s question.

As Nicole put the top down, Marsha covered her head with a scarf to keep her hair from blowing wildly.

"You've never gone for a ride in my car," Nicole said.

"It's beautiful! Inside, and out. And, it still has that new car smell." Nicole tuned the radio to a country station and began singing along with the song playing. It was a short drive to Manny's. She parked beneath a light pole near the front entrance, and the girls took the elevator to the tenth floor. Before they knocked, Manny opened the door greeting them with a smile.

"What happened to you," he asked Marsha, noticing the bruise that she was trying to cover with make-up.

"I should learn not to play with my kids. Sometimes, they get a little rough." Marsha hated lying, especially to Manny. But the truth had no place in their relationship, she reasoned.

On this day, Manny stood over the girls where they lay entwined naked on the bed, thinking about how much he had grown to adore them. He especially enjoyed watching them play with the sex toys Nicole so readily provided. The girls made him feel young again. As long as he had Nicole and Marsha, he no longer needed to look for the Fountain of Youth. There was something special about the feisty little shit, Nicole. She had dug her way deep into his heart. Whatever she wanted was hers for the asking, but she never asked for anything. She seemed to only want to please him in any way possible. Never once had she tried to take advantage of his kind nature.

What Nicole would never know was in the event of his death, he was leaving all of his worldly possessions to her. Only two people were aware of this fact, him and his attorney. Manny felt good about leaving her an estate that would be quite substantial.

* * *

Betty Crawford had a new and promising lead. Her informant said the last time anyone had seen Missy was three days before she was fished out of the Harbor. She was last seen around three o' clock in the morning at the Wee Hours. It wasn't very much information, but it was more than they had.

Detective Marks twisted the cigar in his mouth, rolling it from one side to the other. "Keep up the good work, Twinkle Toes," he said. In other words, the information was, for the most part, worthless.

* * *

Detective Hill was livid. Not one, but both Nicole Redman and Detective Daniels had gotten him in hot water with Marsha Bennett. He thought Charlie Redman was an asshole, but he expected nothing from him, especially after busting his head against a door frame. Where was Nicole? What was the 'Fuck You' note she left behind all about? On top of everything else, his investigations were going nowhere. The thing to do, he decided, was to return to square one.

After obtaining a photo of Harold Bennett, he returned to the Blue Onion to question Tony and the dancers a second time. It was nine o'clock when he parked in front of the Blue Onion, The door was propped open. There weren't many patrons, but the night was still early. Tony was standing outside near the front door rolling a quarter through his fingers, then flipping it into the air before catching it.

Nicole spotted the dark blue Ford Maverick from her place inside the dim interior of the bar as it parked. Before Detective Hill stepped out of the car, she told Stormy to come get her when the cop left, then hurried down the hallway to the girl's powder room.

"You got a minute?" Detective Hill asked Tony as he approached.

"As you can see I'm pretty busy," Tony snickered.

"I would like to show you and the girls a photo of Harold Bennett to see if they recognize him?"

"Let me see the photo," Tony said. He glanced at the offered photo and immediately started shaking his head. "Nope, he doesn't look familiar."

"Mind if I ask the girls inside?" Hill asked, not really caring if the other man gave his permission, or not. He was going inside no matter what.

"As long as you pay the two dollar cover charge you can ask them anything you want."

Sergeant Hill frowned, then paid the two dollar cover charge. Once inside he soon learned that none of the girls recognized Harold Bennett. Hill stepped outside to where Tony still sat on a stool.

"Mind if I ask you a few more questions?"

Tony chuckled, then answered the question with a question of his own. "Have you heard the story of the three Monkeys? See no evil. Hear no evil. Say no evil."

Detective Hill's face suddenly turned red with anger. "You want to play games? I'll show you how to play games, punk," he retorted.

"Get the fuck out of here flatfoot! This ain't your friggin' jurisdiction anyway!"

For a brief second Hill thought about slapping the other man off the stool. But that would be very foolish for him to do that. Hill knew he was out of his district and was functioning with no real authority. Frustrated and pissed off, he turned and stepped his way back to his car.

Back inside the bar Stormy opened the bathroom door. "You can come out now, Peaches," she announced, then asked. "What was that all about?"

"I know that cop. He's from the Anne Arundel County Sheriff's Department and he may have a warrant for me. I just thought it best not to take any chances."

"I don't blame you," Stormy laughed.

"What are you doing after work?"

"I don't have any plans. Would you like to go to another after-hour club?"

"There's more?"

"There's three. Susies, Hectors, and the Wee Hours. The Wee Hours is the most popular. We've been there and you've met the owner, Gus. Dick and Jerry Everhart own Hectors. Some old lady owns Susies."

"Let's go to Hectors." Peaches smiled.

"Hectors, it is!" Stormy smiled back.

* * *

When Jerry spotted Stormy walking through the door of Hectors it was three o'clock in the morning. From previous visits he was well acquainted with the dancer known as Stormy, but the platinum blonde she was with was completely unknown to him. He immediately asked who Nicole was.

"That's Peaches." Stormy replied smiling. "She's a dancer at the Blue Onion."

"She's a looker. Does she work the streets?" Jerry asked.

"No, she's a decent girl!"

"I like all girls," Jerry grinned.

Nicole walked over and stood beside Stormy. Jerry gave her a quick once over before introducing himself. "Hi! I'm Jerry. My brother and I own this place. If you need anything, let me know?"

"Thank you," Nicole smiled sweetly.

* * *

Detective Hill called a close friend who worked as a reporter for the Baltimore Sun newspaper and asked for a favor.

"Sure, anything for you, Dave."

* * *

Tony Bedsoe wiped the sleep from his eyes, climbed out of bed, and slowly slipped on a bathrobe and house slippers. His morning ritual never varied. He walked to the front door of his two bedroom home, opened the door, and retrieved the morning newspaper. The newspaper boy delivered the Baltimore Sun daily. On the handlebar of the delivery boys bicycle was a basket filled with newspapers. He grabbed a paper and slung it with one hand landing it squarely on the front doorstep, never missing his intended target. Tony grabbed the newspaper and stepped back inside his house tossing the newspaper on top of the kitchen table. He opened a loaf of bread and dropped two slices into the toaster, then made a cup of coffee adding milk and two sugars. When the toast popped up, he buttered it generously. As he stirred the coffee, he listened to the cling and clang against the sides of the cup. He took a sip of the hot coffee, then reached for the morning paper and unwrapped it. He was hit by the headlines which read: BALTIMORE MOBSTER TELLS ALL. As Tony read the article he choked and spat his coffee out in a spray of liquid. "Mutha fucker!"

Tony yelled. He quickly dressed, then spent the next two hours going from one phone booth to another frantically calling everyone and telling that it was a lie, he never cooperated with the police.

Stormy was just waking up when Nicole called and asked, "Did you see this morning's paper?"

"No, why?"

The headline is BALTIMORE MOBSTER TELL ALL. The story says that Tony Bedsoe, the manager of the Blue Onion on Howard Street cooperated fully in the murder investigation of Harold Bennett."

"You're shittin' me!" Stormy said, jumping up from her bed.

Domonic Coroza was sitting in a restaurant sipping on a cup of black coffee and eating a jelly filled donut when he read the headlines, then the story. "That son of a bitch," he swore aloud.

CHAPTER THIRTEEN

RIDE THE WIND

Leaving the motel Juice drove to Mango's, his favorite nightclub in Miami. He generously tipped the Hostess and asked for a booth near the ladies powder room. That was the spot to be, he thought. It offered a view of the girls coming and going as well as the ones on the dance floor. The red leather couch where they were seated was shaped like a half moon and a round glass table sat before them. After ordering drinks, Juice laid out four lines of cocaine on the glass table, snorted two, and passed the straw to Charlie. The gesture attracted passing girls like moths to a flame. They drank, partied, and danced with beautiful girls until closing time.

In Baltimore, Charlie was accustomed to going bar hopping. Going from one bar to the next, drinking and putting dollar bills into dancers' garter belts. A few bars had a band and a dance floor. But the nightclub scene in Miami was First Class and nothing like he had ever known.

The following morning they checked out of the Holiday Inn and drove back to Naples. Charlie bid his friend a quick goodbye with an embrace and slap on the back. He drove to the airport, returned the rental car, and caught the first flight to Baltimore.

Charlie was glad to be home and he was already making plans to rent a house. It had to set off to itself, so people could come and go without attracting attention. He also needed a safe place to stash the fifty kilo's of pure cocaine. During the flight, he made a list of everything he needed to do knowing that he would need a mask, a scale, and packaging material. Juice was to be his man in Florida. When he was prepared to receive his first delivery, he had been instructed to call Juice. But they hadn't discussed how to transport the money.

Charlie wondered how in the fuck was he going to move such a large quantity of cocaine? He was clueless. But he told himself that he was going to make it happen or die trying. At the top of his list was 'guns'. He would need guns for protection. He purchased a .357

Ruger with a six inch barrel, and a snub nose Charter Arms 38. He knew that he would need better weapons, but those would do for now.

* * *

When Detective Daniels arrived at work he asked, "Who did Tony Bedsoe cooperate with? What information did he divulge? Was there a deal made through the prosecutor's office, and were there any arrest warrants issued?"

Everyone had read the article and they were looking at each other equally dumbfounded. Detective Daniels placed a call to the Baltimore Sun and asked to speak with the reporter who had written the article. His call was transferred to the reporter's desk.

"Good morning, Jack Trepper. How may I help you?"

"This is Detective Daniels from the Baltimore County Sheriffs Department. I'm calling in regards to an article you wrote for this morning edition. The issue about the Baltimore Mobster."

"Yes."

"Where did you get your information from?"

"I'm sorry, but that's confidential and privileged information."

"I'm in charge of the investigation, for Christ sake!"

"I'm sorry, but I'm not permitted to reveal my sources. I can connect you to our legal department if you wish."

Detective Daniels slumped back in his chair and replied, "Kiss my ass!" and hung up the phone.

* * *

Sergeant Hill grinned from ear to ear when he opened the morning paper and read the headline. It was more than he had hoped for. He would have been satisfied with a much smaller article in the Second Section.

* * *

Normally Tony lounged on a stool outside the front door of the club, going through his bit with the quarter rolling over his fingers. Tonight it was different. He sat just inside the doorway collecting the two dollar cover charge, alert to every movement. In the small of his back he stuck a Walther 9mm PPK, careful to keep it beneath his jacket and out of sight. Under the jacket Tony wore a white turtleneck sweater, dark blue pants, and black leather Italian loafers with tassels.

Tony suddenly heard the unmistakable roar of a group of Harley Davidson motorcycles as a small band of bikers rode into view. They slowed to a complete stop, then one by one walked their bikes backwards until the rear tire touched the curb. Bikers always backed their bikes up because it looked cool and it made for a faster getaway. There were four bikers wearing colors. They were 'Argots'. Tony knew enough about biker patches to know that the biggest biker was a Sergeant of Arms. He also knew the Argots were a biker club out of Pennsylvania and the upper rocker on their black leather jackets confirmed it, putting Tony automatically on high alert. Their headquarters was rumored to be a cabin in the woods of Pennsylvania. In the six years he had managed the bar he had never had a crew of bikers come in. They were known to manufacture and sell crystal meth.

"What's the cover charge?" the Sergeant asked Tony.

"That's not for you guys." Tony smiled, hoping to live through the night.

The bikers filed past Tony, going to belly up to the bar and order large mugs of beer.

Nicole soon replaced the large breasted Amber on top of the bar. She strutted her stuff while looking at the black leather jackets with interest. They were a group of bearded unsavory looking characters who drank and grinned a lot. They soon became loud, sometimes obnoxious, but something about them turned Nicole on. Tony remained by his place at the door watching both the bikers and the street at the same time.

"What's your name, honey?" the big biker asked.

"Peaches," she smiled.

"Well, I'd like to eat a Peach," he laughed.

Nicole continued to dance, smiling down at him. "What's your name," she asked shyly.

"Bulldog! I'm the leader of this pack."

When the music stopped Nicole sat down next to Bulldog and asked him to buy her a drink.

"Sure, Peaches. What are you drinking?"

Sassy replaced Nicole on top of the bar, her long dark hair swinging from side to side as she swirled her narrow hips from side to side. The beat in the bar went up a notch. "Champagne," she leaned over to whisper in his ear.

"I'll buy you whatever you want, but if you spit it back into that Seven-Up bottle you'll be spitting out your teeth too."

"I'll drink it," Nicole giggled, not taking offense. "It's hot in here. I need to step outside for a minute and get some fresh air. Which one of those motorcycles is yours?"

"The white one."

Nicole grabbed a thin T-shirt from behind the bar before stepping outside. She took a moment to admire the motorcycles paying particular attention to the pearl white one, it had a lot of chrome and sparkled under the neon lights. On the rear fender there was a pair of black saddlebags with leather fringes and a small black padded seat.

"That's a sissy seat."

Nicole spun around finding Bulldog standing behind her. He moved real quiet for being such a big man.

"It's for the old lady," he explained, pointing to the foot pegs. "And that's where the old lady puts her feet."

"You take your mother with you," she asked,

Bulldog laughed. "An old lady is your main squeeze. She's your momma, or, your property."

Below the small metal license plate hung a plastic plague that read: 'Ass or Gas - Nobody rides for free'. After reading it, Peaches laughed. In the dimness of the bar it had been hard to see him, but outside the bar beneath the lights she could see him much more clearly. He stood six feet tall, weighing an estimated two hundred and fifty pounds. He had shoulder length brown hair, a full beard, and his teeth were surprisingly white. Bulldog handed her a baggy containing a white powder and instructed "Go snort some of this."

Peaches went back inside, very much aware of Tony watching her every move. She made her way quickly to the powder room, with the baggy clutched tightly in her little fist. She laid out two lines and snorted one line into each nostril. She immediately felt a burning sensation, then a rush that scared her. After a few seconds she felt like the blood was rushing through her veins, and she hurriedly left the bathroom. Her eyes were wide open and she felt like she was racing to get back outside to where Bulldog stood waiting. She knew that what she had just snorted was not cocaine.

"What was that you gave me," she asked, feeling like she could dance for days.

"Crystal Meth. It will make your clitty litter."

Peaches giggled. "I wanna go for a ride on the back of your Harley, and I don't have any money."

Bulldog thought he knew exactly what the little bitch was implying and he was all too happy to oblige her.

Peaches looked over at Tony. "Is it okay if I go for a ride?"

"Sure, Peaches. No problem." Tony said, suddenly feeling better. The bikers might not be there for him after all.

Nicole's nipples were clearly visible and as hard as rocks through the thin T-shirt. She straddled the bike wearing a g-string and flip-flops, wrapping her arms around Bulldog's waist as the bike roared to life. Soon they shot down the street, the vibrations of the engine tickling her pussy. It felt good. She suddenly wanted some dick, and she assumed it was the drugs kicking in. Her hair blew wildly in the wind giving her a sense of freedom. She grabbed Bulldog's crotch and felt his manhood rising.

Bulldog raced down several streets in search of a secluded place, his hunger for the little blonde growing with each passing second. Finally, he pulled the bike behind a closed factory, parked, and killing the engine lifted Nicole off the back of the bike. He yanked down her skimpy g-string, spun her around and bent her over, exposing her moist, warm, pussy. He dropped his jeans to his knees and shoved his eight and a half inches into her tight pussy. He held her up off the ground by her hips and Nicole found herself clutching onto the seat of the motorcycle for balance while he rammed into her without mercy. Peaches cried out her shock and pleasure at his forcefulness. It was sheer ecstasy! When Bulldog shot his load, he trembled. Damn this bitch is hot and she has one tight pussy, he thought. From inside his saddle bags he gave her some tissue to clean both of them off. When she once again wore her g-string and his pants were pulled up, they stood there smiling at one another. Now that the sex was over, Peaches only had one question.

"How do I get more crystal meth?"

"It's the poor man's drug. I can sell it to you for three hundred dollars an ounce," he offered, handing Peaches a card with his phone number on it. "I'm generally there and awake around noon."

"Can I purchase some now?"

"I will ask my brothers if they have any with them for sale."

When they returned to the bar, Tony was still sitting on the stool inside the doorway. They walked past him to the bar and Bulldog took a second to introduce her to his brothers Jammer, Cupcake, and Kapote. Then he asked them if they had any crystal meth with them. Jammer had an eighth of an ounce, which he offered to Peaches as a gift.

"Thank you!" Peaches beamed, while discreetly putting away the package he slipped to her.

"Give me a call," Bulldog grinned. "We have some business to take care of and only stopped by for a quick drink."

Peaches smiled. She liked Bulldog and she knew he liked her too. She smiled as she watched the group of rough men exit the bar and walk past Tony. The smile on her face turned to a frown at the sight of Tony's dour looking face.

All of the dancers and barmaids noticed that Tony had been acting strange since the article appeared in the newspaper. He rarely played with the quarter or stood outside the bar. What exactly was it that was worrying him, Peaches wondered. It was obvious he was worried about something, or someone.

Later near closing time Stormy asked Peaches if she wanted to hit the circuit with her after work. The circuit meant making a round to all three of the after-hour clubs. Hectors, Susies, and the Wee Hours. Peaches was feeling wired. The drugs had her feeling thirsty. She was grinding her teeth and both sides of her jaw were aching. Her pupils were dilated to the size of dimes. Wide awake, she was ready for some action. Of course she wanted to go hangout with Stormy. But she told herself that next time, she would only do one line of Crystal Meth. After work they made their way outside and around the corner to where Stormy's yellow Pontiac convertible was parked. They quickly put the top down. The early morning was quiet with only an occasional car driving past.

"Are you high?" Stormy asked.

"Hell yeah," Peaches laughed. "You want some?"

"Some of what?"

"Crystal Meth."

"You've got Meth? Of course I want some. How did you get it?"

Peaches grabbed the baggy from her purse while Stormy removed a compact mirror from her own purse. Peaches had no intentions of telling her where she got the Crystal Meth. Stormy flipped open her compact mirror, rolled up a dollar bill, and snorted a line. Her eyes lit up and she snapped. "This is some good shit! The best I've ever had!"

Peaches smiled, pleased by Stormy's report.

"Let's not go to the Wee Hours first."

"Why not," Peaches asked.

"Gus hates drugs. He would take one look at the two of us, throw our asses out, and bar us forever."

"Why does he hate drugs so much?"

"I don't know. I just know how he is. He meant what he told you. Don't ever go into club using drugs, with drugs, or attempt to sell drugs in his club. So where do you want to go first, Susies or Hectors?"

As Stormy pulled away from the curb, Peaches said, "Susies." Peaches liked feeling the wind blowing through her hair, but nothing compared to her riding the bitch seat on the back of Bulldog's Harley. She wondered where he was and what he was doing.

* * *

Bulldog and his crew were ten miles away in Sparrow's Point, and outside of a bar called the Eagle's Nest. They were anxiously waiting for one of the bouncers to get off work. The bouncer had physically thrown Rooster out of the bar for patting one of the dancers on the ass. Rooster was wearing his Club colors when the incident occurred, so there was no excuses to be made. When you fuck over a brother Argot, you have all of them to deal with. Bulldog reasoned the bouncer would have plenty of time to reflect on his poor judgment while he was laying in a hospital bed recovering from the ass kicking that he was about to receive, courtesy of Bulldog.

The bouncer responsible for physically tossing Rooster from the bar would be easy to recognize. Rooster described the man as being six feet four inches in height, weighing two hundred pounds, and his blonde hair was cut in a Mohawk. He would stand out in a crowd.

CHAPTER FOURTEEN

THE BIG BANG

Peaches was unimpressed by the atmosphere at Susies afterhour club. There was a much older crowd and there was no real action going on. It was a quiet place where many of the city's bartenders dropped in to unwind. Peaches and Stormy were flying higher than a kite and were prepared to party all night long. They quickly left Susies and headed for Hectors.

When Jerry Everhart saw the girls coming through the front door he told the bouncer at the door, "No cover charge!" and personally escorted them to a table. The place was 'poppin' as Peaches liked to call it. She was wearing tight fitting jeans, a white T-shirt showing off pointy nipples, and her ever present flip-flops. Her fingernails and toenails were freshly polished a hot pink.

"Do you see what I just put in?" Jerry asked, standing beside their table.

The after-hour club was a large room with a circular bar located dead center against the far rear wall. Access to the rear rooms could be gained by moving past the small dance floor to the left of the bar. On the right side of the bar stood a small stage, and on that stage now stood a brand new stripper pole. At the sight of the pole Stormy laughed and Peaches' eyes went wide. Peaches had never performed on a stripper pole and at that moment she was game for anything as long as it was fun. All of the tables and booths before the bar were packed with drinking and laughing patrons, but no one seemed to be interested in the new pole.

"Have you ever been on a stripper pole," she asked Stormy excitedly.

"I grew up on one! " Stormy bragged with a laugh. "Put some money in the jukebox, Jerry."

Jerry was more than happy to oblige. Stormy got up to go climb onto the stage. She immediately went into a twirl around the pole, both hands grasping high on the bar, and her legs leaving the floor.

Peaches watched as Stormy rocked the pole dirty dancing, her moves drawing the attention of the packed room. Stormy threw her legs in the air, wrapped them around the pole and slowly spun herself down, her actions receiving the applause of the room. Then it was Peaches turn to show her stuff. She started off slow and easy, but was soon working the pole like a seasoned pro. She threw her legs in the air, wrapped them around the pole and spun herself down.

"Not bad," Stormy clapped along with the crowd.

Jerry kept putting quarters in the jukebox and the girls took turns performing. Everyone was enjoying the show and Jerry could not wait to tell his brother Dick that the pole was the best investment they could have made. When they were once again seated at the table with drinks of champagne, Peaches decided to question Jerry.

"I hear you're a pimp," she asked.

"Who told you that?"

"I hear things," she smiled.

"Are you interested in going to work for me?"

"Nope, but would you show me your office?"

Jerry escorted her to his office, located through a door behind the bar. Peaches closed the door behind them, unzipped his pants and sucked him off right there inside the cluttered small office. In less than a couple minutes he shot his load.

Peaches cleaned him up with her tongue then climbed to her feet with a bright smile. "I just wanted you to know that your girls ain't shit compared to me," she tucked him back inside his pants, then walked laughing from the room.

Jerry stood there speechless, feeling drained and used. He hated to admit it but she was the best cock-sucker he had ever met and he had known a lot of them!

* * *

It was four o'clock in the morning when Tony Bedsoe pulled into his driveway and parked. He looked around to make sure no one was hiding in some dark place or behind a bush to ambush him. Satisfied that the coast was clear he stepped out of the car, quickly locked the door, hurried to the front door, unlocked it and stepped inside. Immediately he smelled a strange odor and flipped the light switch on next to the door, hoping to investigate the source. The last thing Tony heard was a roar, never understanding that it was a massive explosion that ended his life.

Four hours earlier, Domonic had forced open the back door of the house, searching out and turning off the pilot lights to the furnace and gas stove. He tapped on the bulb of the lamp in the living room until it burst, careful not to break the filament. Then he disconnected the gas line to the stove allowing the house to fill up with natural gas. He set two five gallon cans of gasoline on the kitchen floor and left. Domonic had been told that a gallon of gas was the equal of two sticks of dynamite, so ten gallons would easily be the equivalent of twenty sticks. Nobody was going to snitch on Domonic Coroza and live to tell about it.

When Tony flipped on the light switch, it created a spark igniting the natural gas. The explosion rattled windows in houses a block away.

Tony had two sisters, both married. One lived in Boise, Idaho, the other one somewhere in New Jersey. Nobody knew how to get in touch with them and Tony had no real friends to speak of. His body was cremated and a small obituary appeared in the Baltimore Sun. There was no funeral or memorial service. Nicole felt that Tony was somehow involved with the assault on Jeff Miles, her daughter's death, and the murder of Harold Bennett. She had no sympathy for the bastard! What was upsetting was the Blue Onion was closed while the owner looked for a new manager. She had never met or seen the owner and she wondered who owned the bar.

* * *

Nicole's special ordered license plate finally arrived in the mail. It simply read 'PEACHES' in big bold letters. She decided to pay a visit to Charlie's apartment. She wanted to stop by and surprise him with a introduction to crystal meth. Stormy had informed her that it was also known by another name, crank.

Charlie opened the door and invited her inside. He was packing up as if he was getting ready to move. There were already filled boxes stacked close beside the door.

"Where are you moving to Charlie," she demanded.

"I rented a house."

"Where?"

"In White Marsh. It's about fifteen minutes on the other side of the harbor tunnel."

"Were you planning to tell me?"

"Nicole, I have no way of getting in touch with you. If you stopped by I intended on telling you. I'm moving! There, I've told you."

"Are you moving in with someone?"

"No," Charlie laughed. He knew that she meant was he moving in with another woman.

"Have you ever tried crystal meth," she asked curiously.

"Once."

"Wanna do a line? It's good. It will keep you going for a long time."

"I have a lot of serious shit on my mind right now. It's not a good time."

"I'll help you pack. Would it interest you if I said I could buy it uncut for three hundred dollars an ounce," she smiled. She knew Charlie was getting a kilo of cocaine a month for the help he provided to a friend.

Charlie turned away from her and walked out onto the balcony. He leaned against the wrought iron railing and admired Nicole's silver Mercedes-Benz. That's when he saw her personalized license plate, and the name 'Peaches'.

"Where did you get that nickname from," he smiled.

"C'mon Charlie, just try one line for me."

"For you?" Charlie grinned.

"Yeah, it will make your dick harder than the rock of Gibralter and you'll be able to fuck for hours."

"Nicole I've got some serious shit happening. You have no idea."

"Charlie, I was married to your stinking ass for six years. During that time you never once ate my pussy. Now that I think about it, you still haven't. But the sex has been better since you started paying for it."

"I've always paid for it, one way or another. Rent, utilities, groceries. When we divorced, I paid friggin' child support. I don't know what makes you think that pussy has ever been free."

Nicole laughed. "That's what I like about you, Charlie. You've always made me laugh."

"C-mon, give me a line." Charlie grinned.

"I'm off work for a week, maybe longer."

"I didn't know you had a job." Charlie frowned.

Nicole had not meant to let that slip. Somehow, it just slipped out.

"I'm a babysitter," she offered. Which was pretty much the truth. She took care of drunken sailors, bikers, degenerates, and one dirty old man whom she absolutely adored.

Charlie snorted the line of crystal meth. He felt the burning sensation and then the sudden rush. "That's some really good stuff!" Within minutes his dick was rock hard and he wanted to fuck Nicole's brains out. He knew she wanted it, too. Charlie looked at Nicole, grinned, and asked, "Do you wanna get lucky?"

"Money up front," she giggled.

"You conniving little bitch," Charlie snapped.

"Like you said, Charlie. It ain't ever been free."

Charlie handed her a eighth of an ounce of cocaine. Then he spent the next hour and a half giving her a good grudge fuck.

Charlie and Nicole lay naked in bed, their legs entwined like pretzels. With their heads resting on pillows they stared into each other eyes. She knew him well enough to know that something was really troubling him and he knew her well enough to know that she would never betray his trust.

It was Nicole's dumb ass luck that caused Charlie to go to prison. He was just a small time dealer who grew marijuana in their basement. Nicole was driving down the road when she was stopped for speeding. She had just smoked a joint and her car wreaked of marijuana and that's what brought the heat down. After a two month investigation the police raided their house. She kept her mouth shut and Charlie took the bust. While he was in prison, she divorced Charlie because she wanted to give their daughter a better life than Charlie was willing to offer. She did not want Charlotte to grow up with memories of visiting her father in prison. It was no secret that Charlie was to scared to steal and too lazy to work. There was never going to be the white picket fence or a pot of gold at the end of his rainbow.

"Do you ever think about Charlotte," she asked, continuing to look into his eyes.

"Sometimes. You need to understand that I was never really in her life. When I went to prison you divorced me. Charlotte was three then. We never had a father and daughter relationship. We never had that bond. I dreamed about coming home, walking through the front door and her running to throw her little arms around my legs. Whenever I do think about Charlotte, I'm sorry that I missed that!" Charlie wiped his eyes trying to hold back the tears. Nicole was consumed with a feeling of guilt. For the first time in her life she realized that everything was not all black and white.

"Why are you moving, Charlie?"

"Business. I need a place that's secluded where no one will notice people coming or going."

Nicole noticed a gun on top of the nightstand next to the bed and asked, "Why do you have a gun, Charlie?"

"I'm not going to let someone rob me."

"Ain't nobody going to rob you. You don't have anything," she laughed.

"There are things you don't know about."

"Enlighten me. I'm a good listener. If I can help you, I will."

Charlie confided in Nicole without mentioning any names or elaborating. He had fifty kilos of cocaine coming and no buyers. At first she thought Charlie was lying to her. It was hard to imagine someone fronting him fifty kilos of cocaine.

"How much is it costing you for a kilo?"

"Eighteen thousand. I should be able to sell them for twenty eight thousand; forty in New York!"

"Here I thought I was going to impress you with my crystal meth connection," Nicole laughed.

"I was given a nickname to use when I sell drugs."

"What is it?"

"Peanut."

Nicole laughed heartily. "It fits you, Charlie."

"By the way, your cop boyfriend called looking for you."

"What did you tell him?"

"I told him you had platinum blonde hair, were driving a new Mercedes, and that I fucked your brains out. Then I hung up the phone."

"I bet he thought you were full of shit," she giggled.

Nicole finished helping Charlie pack, then they exchanged phone numbers and addresses.

"By the way, he's not my boyfriend." Nicole announced as she left the apartment.

Charlie grinned.

CHAPTER FIFTEEN

BIKERS PARADISE

Nicole parked her Mercedes in the underground garage at Regency Towers. put the top up, locked the doors, and turned the alarm on. Then, she carefully pulled the custom protective cover over it, as if she was putting her child to bed. She said goodnight to her beloved Bug parked beside the Mercedes, then took the elevator to her upstairs apartment.

Even though she had no plans for visitors, and never thought of it as home, she kept her place to retreat immaculate. As she entered her bedroom, she picked up her Rolodex from the bed side table and thumbed through the names. Her collection of numbers was very limited. There was Detective Hill's, the Blue Onion, Manny's condo, Marsha's, and Stormy's phone numbers. She added Charlie and Bulldog's phone numbers to her Rolodex, then dialed the number for Bulldog.

"Argots forever, forever Argots. This is Jammer. What can I do for you?"

"Hi. This is Peaches. Is Bulldog in?"

"Hey Peaches. I remember you from the bar. Kinda hard to forget your fine little ass. Bulldog was out back. Let me check and see if he still is."

About five minutes later, a familiar voice came over the line. "Peaches baby. How are you?" Bulldog asked. Normally, when someone called for him, there was a problem.

"I'm good. But the Blue Onion is closed until they find a new manager. Someone blew Tony's house up with him inside. I've got nothing to do and I'm bored."

"Hey! We're throwing a party this weekend at the cabin. Would you like to come?"

"Not me. I've heard stories about how you bikers run trains on girls and I don't intend to fuck the entire club."

"I'll tell you what I'll do. For the day, I'll make you my old lady.

If you are wearing my patch no one will disrespect you. It will be a lot of fun, but it does get a little wild."

"What should I wear?"

"Most of the old ladies wear jeans, T-shirts or tank tops, and boots. There's going to be a wet T-shirt contest and mud wrestling."

"I'm not mud wrestling!" Peaches retorted.

"You don't have to." Bulldog chuckled, then gave her the directions to the cabin. It was fifteen miles outside of the City of Harrisburg, Pennsylvania on a hundred acres.

* * *

It was a beautiful morning and the sun was just coming over the horizon when Peaches uncovered the silver Mercedes-Benz and put the convertible top down. She stopped at a convenience store to fill the gas tank and purchase a pint of orange juice. Then she sat down in the driver's seat, opened the center console, and searched for her sunglasses. After a moments search, she realized that she had left them laying on the kitchen table at the apartment, so she rushed back inside the store and selected a cheap pair of sunglasses from a rack. The frames were pink and they only cost three dollars. After paying the cashier, she went back out to her car and drove north, having been informed the drive would be at a minimum four hours.

She turned the radio up, sang loudly, and drummed on the dash board. There was no one listening or watching, and singing to herself made her feel more vibrant and alive.

As Peaches drove out of the City of Harrisburg and into the country she started seeing more and more bikers wearing black leather jackets with the Argot patch. She remembered how she had felt riding bitch on the back of Bulldog's Harley and envied every girl riding on the sissy seat. As she neared the front gated entrance leading to the bikers headquarters she became aware of a sudden escort. Two bikers raced their motorcycles around in front of the Mercedes and four pulled in behind. As they passed beyond a wide open wooden gate and onto a gravel road Peaches was slowly becoming enraged, assuming the bikers did not know that she was Bulldog's guest. The Mercedes sped along the road for a short time, then a small ranch style log cabin came into view. Knowing that Bulldog was expecting her, she started honking the horn repeatedly. Surely he would come outside to greet her, she thought. The car skidded to a stop in an area dominated by other vehicles and motorcycles, and a number of big burley bikers surrounded the car.

"Hey momma, did you make a wrong turn?" A bearded biker reached through the open car window and grabbed a handful of titty as he tried to kiss her.

Jammer was in the crowd of bikers and at first he did not recognize Peaches as being the driver of the Mercedes, but catching a brief glimpse of the vanity plate that read 'Peaches' he shouted at his brothers. "Back the fuck off!"

The biker that had reached into the car received a hard smack from Nicole which sent him into a fit of laughter. At the call from Jammer, the bikers slowly backed away from the car making her feel like the Queen of the prom. Now, if only her Prince Charming would show his face. She climbed out of the car.

"Where's Bulldog," she demanded.

"He had a rough night," Rooster chuckled. "I don't think he's out of bed yet."

"Can't say I blame him," Cupcake chuckled.

"There's room for one more," Rooster grinned.

"Where's his bedroom?" Peaches snapped.

"Through the front door, last door on the left," Jammer grinned. Peaches stomped off towards the cabin and the crowd of bikers parted to let her through.

"This is going to be good!" Jammer looked around at his fellow bikers, and with a wave of his hand they begin to follow after Peaches.

Peaches walked inside the cabin making a bee-line for Bulldog's bedroom. She flung open the bedroom door. Bulldog was laying on top of the covers butt naked with a scooter tramp under each arm. Scooter tramps were considered the lowest of the low. One of the bitches was asleep with her hand wrapped around his dick.

Peaches screamed out a long string of obscenities and the trio woke up in startled surprise. Peaches grabbed the first bitch that she could get her hands on and yanked her from the bed, making her ass hit the floor with a thud. She grabbed the other tramp by her hair and drug her from the bed, pounding her head with a flurry of fists.

Bulldog was dazed and confused as he rubbed the sleep from his eyes. The brothers were laughing and enjoying the show. It took Bulldog a second to shake the sleep from his eyes.

"Peaches, what the fuck?" Bulldog yelled.

Peaches stepped back away from the second female. "You said that today I'm your old lady. I'm claiming my territory. If you've got a problem with that, I'll leave."

Bulldog suddenly grinned. "No problem."

Several bikers quickly escorted the two dazed biker tramps from the room. Bulldog left the room to take a shower and get dressed. Word quickly spread about Peaches, her new Mercedes, and how she kicked the two bitches' asses. Brothers were soon recognizing Peaches by her Platinum blonde hair.

If they were going to get together later that night, it damn sure wasn't going to be between the sheets used by those tramps, Peaches swore to herself as she changed the bedding. The tramps weren't even pretty, she thought. One had a beer belly, and the other had ugly teeth and sagging breasts. They were nothing for her to be jealous of.

After Bulldog dressed, he handed Peaches a girl's black leather jacket. It had the Argot colors on the back and across the front a patch that read, 'Property of Bulldog'. There was not a swinging dick within a hundred miles that would dare to fuck with her now.

"What's that awful smell," she asked as they stepped outside the cabin.

"It's from the Crystal Meth lab. Believe it or not, that's a half mile back in the woods. If you think it smells bad here, you should walk back there."

"I'll pass! But I have some business to discuss with you later."

"It's time for us to join the party," Bulldog grinned giving her a wet kiss.

The club had purchased ten kegs of beer and one hundred cases of Budweiser for a party of 200 members, their old ladies and guests, and they were still uncertain if it would be enough beer. Aluminum wash tubs were filled with ice to keep the beer cold, and every two hours a truck went into town and brought back more bags of ice.

Bikers gathered at a steep hill where some tried to ride their motorcycles to the top. Dirt flew in every direct ion as one biker after another accepted the challenge. In the middle of the yard was a very old rusted Harley Davidson that was known as a 'rat bike'. It was made before World War II, and to the biker community it was considered an icon.

The bikers were going wild. They tied a rope to an old tire and tied the other end to a Harley. A biker sat on the tire and the Harley raced around, pulling the tire and rider through a field. Another Harley pulled a sled with a rider, while a third pulled a brother wearing water skis. Brothers were doing burn-outs on their Harleys while others were spinning around in circles, doing donuts. Two brothers dressed up like knights and tried to joust on their iron horses.

A group of brothers started bonfires and threw a stolen Honda on top of the pile. It was a tradition to burn a Japanese bike. At four o'clock in the afternoon the grills were fired up, cooking mostly hot dogs and hamburgers. In two stainless steel trash cans they cooked a Hobo dinner, consisting of polish sausages, baked potatoes, and corn on the cob.

There was a buffet of drugs inside the house. Bowls filled with crystal meth, cocaine, marijuana, and an assortment of pills. There were big green capsules, little red ones, and solid black pills. In addition, there was a huge pile of white pills with little crosses on them.

Peaches had never drank beer. She never cared all that much for alcohol. But if she wanted to party with the bikers, she knew she would have to learn to hold her liquor. By midnight, she was drunk as a skunk. Bulldog carried her to his bedroom, then returned to join the party.

The following morning, she awoke with one arm and a leg laying over Bulldog's big body. She had a splitting headache, and her mouth was as dry as cotton.

"What happened?" she groaned.

Bulldog stirred beside her. "That's what happens when you drink too much. It happened to me the night before last."

Peaches moaned. She felt like someone had hit her in the head with a sledge hammer.

"Poor baby." Bulldog patted her ass. "I hate to be the bearer of bad news, but the bro's roasted a pig in the back seat of your Mercedes last night."

Peaches shot out of the bed like a rocket, grabbed Bulldog's jacket, wrapped it around her bare ass, and ran out of the bedroom to the front door of the cabin, passing sleeping bodies sprawled across the front room. She snatched open the solid wood door, and looked outside. Her Mercedes had survived the night unscathed. She huffed back to the bed room to find Bulldog rolling on the bed in a fit of laughter.

"Asshole," she darted her piercing eyes toward him, while climbing back onto the bed.

Bulldog grabbed her in his arms. "Next week we're doing a toy run for kids. Do you want to ride bitch?"

"Of course. What kind of Harley is that you have?"

"It's a 1949 Panhead. The engine has been bored forty over with a roller cam and it's been converted to a four speed."

"It looks brand new," Peaches smiled, snuggling close against him.

"It's a new pearl white paint job and I added the chrome accessories."

"I like it."

"I'm glad you do," Bulldog grinned.

Peaches smiled. "Well, it's time to talk business."

"About what?"

"How many kilos of cocaine can the club move in a month?"

"How many do you want me to move?"

"Fifty! I will sell them to you at twenty-eight thousand a kilo un-cut."

"Are you serious?"

"I don't play games when it comes to business or money."

"I will talk to the president of the club, and then I'll get back to you."

"I suggest you do it quick. I'm going to have the fifty kilos soon and I'm looking for someone who can move that large quantity every month."

"You better not be blowing smoke up my ass. If I take this to the club president you better be able to deliver."

"I'll deliver," Peaches smiled.

"Give me your address and phone number."

"No problem."

CHAPTER SIXTEEN

THE TWO O'CLOCK CLUB

On Tuesday night, Peaches called Stormy and told her about the weekend she spent at the Argots' cabin in Pennsylvania partying with Bulldog.

"You are one crazy bitch," Stormy laughed. "What are you doing tonight?"

"I don't have anything planned. Let's go to the Two O'Clock Club. I've been hearing so much about it. I'd like to see what it's like for myself." Peaches suggested.

"I met the owner, Blaze Starr, once. I doubt if she would remember me, but she made quite an impression. Her real name is Ann Fleming. I was invited to a party at her house. She throws one Hell of a party!" Stormy laughed. She recalled Blaze, along with some of her inebriated guests, stripping naked and jumping into the pool.

"I'll pick you up around eight o'clock. Is that good with you?"

"Works for me." Stormy replied, ending their conversation.

Nicole dialed Charlie's number. After three rings, she heard a familiar "Hello."

"We need to get together tomorrow. It's business. I think you're going to be very happy when you hear what I have to say."

"When and where?" was all Charlie asked.

"I will call around noon and we will decide on a time and place to meet. Does that work for you?"

"It works for me." Charlie answered. "How do you like your new place?"

"It sucks being so far out in the boondocks. There's nothing to do and I'm bored to death."

"I understand why you thought you needed to move there, but I don't think it was necessary. I can hardly wait to talk to you, Charlie. I'll call you around noon tomorrow."

"Have a nice day."

"You too," Nicole smiled to herself.

* * *

Peaches picked Stormy up driving the Mercedes and they were parked in front of the Two O'Clock Club by eight-thirty. The cover charge was not in effect until after nine. When they walked through the front door, Blaze Starr was sitting on a stool at the bar. She was a stunning woman in her late thirties to early forties with large green eyes, large forty-four double-D breasts, and flaming red hair, which easily explained her name.

"Don't I know you," she asked Stormy as they took seats close beside her at the bar.

"I was at one of your parties about two years ago. I'm Stormy, and this is my friend, Peaches."

Blaze signaled for the bartender. "Andy, give the girls whatever they want to drink on the house," she instructed the handsome looking man.

Peaches was no drinker, so she had no idea what to order. When Stormy ordered a Long Island Iced-Tea, Peaches added, "Make that two!"

When the drinks arrived, Peaches sipped at the drink, and was pleased when she tasted no alcohol. The drink was surprisingly sweet and delicious. She thought it actually tasted like iced-tea. There was a large sitting area to the right of the bar and a somewhat wide stage placed before the many tables and chairs. The place was set up very much like a show hall.

"Are you one of the dancers?" Peaches asked Blaze.

"I'm not a dancer, honey. I'm a performer! At the Two O'Clock Club we perform burlesque."

"What's the difference?" Peaches laughed.

"It's like comparing day to night. In burlesque, the performers start with their clothes on. There's an art to seduction, honey. Some girls have it, while others never will. I've been in this business for twenty years and there's nothing else that I want to do. In most bars, the girls dance go-go and topless. Stick around and I'll show you how burlesque is performed."

Blaze left them alone to enjoy their drinks and small talk. They watched as she walked through a door and disappeared behind the stage. The club was beginning to fill up with nicely dressed men and women, making Peaches firmly aware of the difference between the Two O'Clock Club and the Blue Onion.

A little after nine o'clock the lights went dim, the music became a sultry tempo, and Blaze glided out onto the stage. She wore a huge head dress of long, colorful feathers, red high heels, a ruffled red blouse, and a very short white skirt. As the music beat throughout the room, Blaze's erotic moves seduced the crowd, telling a story with her body. Starting from the top, she unbuttoned her blouse, one button at a time. After removing it completely, she twirled it around her head several times before letting it fall to the stage. Discreetly, a scantily dressed waitress picked it up. Blaze methodically removed her skirt, then her bra. Stripping down to a g-string, the colorful head-dress, and a set of glistening tassels that covered the nipples of her large 44 double-D breasts. By wiggling her God given assets, Blaze made the white tassels spin around in circles. After watching the show, Peaches was able to understand the difference. She agreed that Blaze was indeed a performer.

After her performance Blaze changed clothes and returned to talk with the girls. She sat down on a stool between them and asked Peaches. "So, what do you think about burlesque?"

"It's certainly different. But how do the girls make any money? You didn't wear a garter belt on stage." Peaches asked, looking around at the female staff of the club. No one seemed to be hustling the customers.

Blaze laughed, then explained. "The bartender passes a tip jar around. At the end of the night the tips are split between the performers. There's no hustling drinks! The girls are paid well. They earn three hundred dollars a night plus tips. It's a higher class clientele. Even the sailors tip well!"

"The girls don't hustle drinks?" Peaches said in disbelief.

"They better not! I run a respectful club."

"I heard it's damn near impossible to get a job working in a club on 'the block'." Stormy added.

"That's true. Why, would you like to try burlesque?"

Stormy was already shaking her head. "Not me."

"I would. I'd love to!" Peaches smiled, jumping to her feet at the opportunity to be on stage. Her eyes sparkled with excitement.

"Well, there's no time like the present. If you're serious, you can pick out an outfit and perform after Trisha."

"Where do I go?"

"C'mon, I'll show you." Blaze replied, with a pleased smile. She grabbed Peaches by her hand to escort her backstage. Peaches hesitated to look at Stormy questioningly. Stormy waved her on, indicating by holding up her glass that she would wait at the bar for her return. Blaze took her backstage and pointed to a huge rack of costumes sized to fit a variety of performers. "Pick one." Blaze offered. "Then you can change in my dressing room."

Two outfits caught Peaches eye; a nurse's and fireman's uniform.

"Hurry up, you're next." Blazed urged her. "When Trisha comes off stage you have three minutes. When you hear the music, that's your cue to step out from behind the curtain. It's your time to shine."

Peaches liked the fireman's helmet, so she chose it. Gathering the rest of the outfit in her arms she followed Blaze to her corner dressing room. She quickly changed into the costume, put red lipstick on her lips and a touch of red rouge on her cheeks. She thought this look enhanced her platinum blonde hair. Then she attached red tassels to cover her nipples. The outfit came with a white blouse, a red leather waist length jacket with a matching wrap-around skirt, and a pair of black rubber boots. As she pulled the boots on, she discovered they were two sizes too large, but she wore them anyway. As Trisha walked off the stage and past Peaches, they exchanged smiles. Or did Trisha smirk, Peaches wondered. She heard the music and stepped lively through the curtains as the announcer said, "Give a big hand for our guest performer, Peaches!"

Peaches' entrance onto the stage was sassy, her hips swinging and her steps made on the balls of her feet. From the moment she made her appearance, she sought to own the stage. She unsnapped the jacket from the bottom up, slowly and provocatively, while making a series of twist and turns to ensure everyone in the club enjoyed her performance. She captured the blouse in her hands and popped the snaps, exposing her small, yet firm breast. It was the action that caught everyone's eye. She slowly unwrapped the skirt, squatted, and twirled the skirt high over her head, doing all of the right moves to garnish the applause of the crowd. She moved like a natural, like she was meant to be on a stage dancing. No one would have ever guessed that this was her maiden performance. She knew she had done well when she heard the thunderous applause as she exited the stage. After changing back into her street clothes, she joined Stormy and Blaze at the bar sitting on the empty stool next to Blaze.

"You were amazing!" Stormy gushed proudly.

"Are you sure you've never performed burlesque before, honey?" Blaze asked smiling.

"I just had fun with it," Peaches replied cheerfully.

"Are you sure you don't want to try," Blaze turned to ask Stormy.

"Maybe some other time. I'm not going to compete with that bitch's performance." Stormy laughed, shaking her head from side to side.

Blaze looked back to Peaches. "Whenever you want a job, come see me!" Blaze offered.

Before Peaches could respond, the bartender interrupted their conversation. "A gentleman in the back booth sitting between the other two suits would like to buy you ladies a drink. He asked me to tell Peaches that he really enjoyed her performance."

"Tell him no thanks for me, but I appreciate the offer," Blaze respectfully declined. She never allowed customers to buy her drinks, a rule she had instituted years ago and stuck to it. Stormy accepted the offer, ordering two Long Island iced tea's, one for herself and one for Peaches.

"Who is he?" Peaches asked the bartender. The man was an older, distinguished looking man in his early fifties.

"Marvin Mandell, he's the governor of the State of Maryland. The other two suits are State Police officers assigned to protect him. He comes in about once a month, usually on a weeknight."

The man held up his glass in a salute. Peaches returned the gesture with a smile. "Tell him I said thanks for the drink,"

"T.M.I." Stormy said.

"What does that mean?"

"Too much information."

"I'd certainly do him!" Peaches laughed. "Tell him I'd like to have his business card," she told the bartender. She watched as the Governor wrote something on the back of a card. When the bartender handed it to her she quickly put it in her purse.

"Aren't you going to read what he wrote?" Stormy inquired. "Not now. I don't want to appear to be to interested." Peaches smiled, looking in the direction of the governor.

* * *

Unlike most mornings when Detective Marks arrived for work, this time he walked directly over to Betty Crawford's desk and said. "Twinkle Toes, grab your things. We're going to go to Milllersville this morning and have a chat with the Everhart brothers at their home."

"What changed your mind," she asked, as they walked outside and to his white Cadillac Coupe Deville.

"I don't think that either of the Everhart's would have murdered one of their own girls. We've got nothing, and they may be more resourceful than us. After all, it's their girls who are working the streets."

The brothers lived in a huge red brick home with well cared for gardens, a manicured lawn, with a Olympic pool and tennis court in the backyard. Detective Marks parked in the driveway, walked to the front door, and rang the doorbell. A girl in a pink negligee answered.

"May I help you," she asked, smiling.

"I would like to speak with either Dick or Jerry Everhart." The big man replied, his eyes fighting to stay on the girl's pretty face and not her sensuous curves. Minutes later, Jerry appeared in the doorway dressed in a blue robe that had a prominent insignia on the upper pocket.

"Did you want to speak with me?" Jerry asked, able to peg them as cops immediately.

"Yes, I'm Detective Marks from the Baltimore City Homicide Division, and this is Detective Crawford. We are investigating the murder of one of your girls."

"My girls?" Jerry questioned blankly.

"Sheila Watts. She was also known as 'Missy'. We know that she worked for you, but we aren't here to investigate you. We aren't interested in prostitution and you are not a suspect."

"What exactly is it you want?"

"I want you to listen. I would like to share some information about her death with you. Our investigation is at a dead end. Your girls work the streets, maybe they will hear something."

"I'm all ears." Jerry invited the detectives inside and offered them something to drink. They declined.

"Two young black boys found Missy's body floating in the harbor, her face being badly eaten by crabs. She had been brutally murdered, stabbed repeatedly. We have no suspects. We received an anonymous call telling us her name, the caller was a female. Missy was raped and her assailant screwed her in the rectum. We believe Missy resisted because she had two broken finger nails and blood in her anus indicating a serious struggle occurred. The last known sighting of Missy was at an after-hour club called the Wee Hours at three in the morning."

"Have you interviewed the owner of the Wee Hours?" Jerry asked.

"No. With the lapse in time we didn't feel it would do any good."

"Probably not." Jerry agreed, then asked. "What do you expect me to do?"

"Have your girls ask around. See what you can find out. My hope is that somehow justice will prevail."

Jerry knew what the big man meant by 'somehow.' It went without saying that if Jerry discovered who murdered his girls, he would never turn the information over to the authorities. No, the guy would not get off that easy.

* * *

Charlie was preparing to mow his lawn when Nicole called. The grass was green and much higher than normal. They decided she would come out to his place for their meeting. He gave her directions to his house in White Marsh. Two hours later Peaches pulled into his driveway, and parked. The sight of her seeing him wearing cut-off jeans, a tank top, and sweating profusely amused her. She was laughing quietly as Charlie shut off the mower and walked over to greet her. Wet grass clung to his brown leather sandals and bare feet. He reached to give her a hug and she stepped out of his reach, forcing him to pursue her with his arms open wide and a smile on his face.

"What's the matter, baby? Don't you love me anymore," he laughed.

"You better be nice to me," she shouted, moving further away from him.

"C'mon inside," he dropped his arms. "I'll make us both a glass of ice-tea."

"How do you like it here?"

"It sucks! There's no action. The highlight of my day yesterday was watching a bird make a nest in a tree." Charlie frowned, then added. "I'm thinking about buying a telescope so I will have something to do at night."

"I may have some good news for you," she smiled.

"Baby, I could use some."

"How would you like for me to sell ten kilos of cocaine for you next week at twenty-eight thousand dollars each?"

"That would be fantastic."

"I'm working on a deal now with the Argot motorcycle club out of Pennsylvania."

"Are you fuckin' nuts? What makes you think they won't rip you off?"

"They won't, Charlie. I have a friend who is pretty high up in the organization. We haven't agreed to a price yet, but I asked for the full amount. If I need to negotiate, I can right? I need to know that's okay with you."

"Just help me move the fifty kilos."

"When will they get here?"

"They're here now. Would you like a taste of my personal product?"

"Give me two eighths. One for me and one to offer the club as a sample of the product."

Nicole followed Charlie into the house where he presented her with the cocaine. She snorted two lines, tilted her head back and sniffed hard. "Damn Charlie, this is some good shit! I'm impressed."

"It's from Peru, Nicole. It's called Peruvian Pink. Notice how it flakes right off the kilo."

* * *

"I think you might want to take a look at this," a junior detective reported to Detective Daniels. "We just got the ballistic report from the lab. The forty-five automatic found in the glove compartment of Tony Bedsoe's car and the forty five bullets taken from Harold Bennett's body are a match. Forensics also matched the tire cast made at the scene of the murder to Bedsoe's car," he handed the report to Daniels.

"Good job. Well, I guess that closes that case."

Detective Daniels decided to call Marsha Bennett and report that Tony Bedsoe was the person responsible for her husband's murder.

"Why did he do it?" Marsha inquired.

"We don't know."

It was the one question no one had an answer for.

* * *

Wednesday morning Nicole met Marsha at her house. As she walked through the front door, Marsha warned, "Watch out for the extension cords!"

Christmas was just around the corner, and Marsha had five children. She was getting an early start on organizing the lights and ornaments, but she did not waste any time talking about the Christmas decorations and got right to the point.

"Your boss killed Harold!" Marsha frowned from her position on the living room floor.

"Tony? How do you know that?"

"A gun was found in the glove compartment of his car. Ballistics matched the bullets that killed Harold to that gun. Tony's car tire tracks also matched to tire tracks found at the scene. Somehow, I think Harold found out that I was seeing Jeff Miles. The big goof probably thought that I was having an affair, so he hired someone to fuck him up." Marsha broke down and cried.

"You don't know that for sure," Nicole offered, hugging Marsha.

"He withdrew twenty-five hundred dollars from the bank shortly after it happened," Marsha explained, believing her theory to be absolutely true. Nicole tried to comfort Marsha. They were family, but there were no words that she could find to help make things easier. So she tried to change the subject. "Are we going to see Manny today?"

"Of course!" Marsha smiled, wiping away her tears.

Nicole looked forward to their seeing Manny. The trio always had a great time.

* * *

Friday night Nicole went to the Two O'Clock Club. As she walked in she saw Blaze sitting at the bar. She sat down on a stool next to her and said, "If that job offer is still open, I can start Monday night."

"Then I guess I'll see you Monday, Peaches." Blaze smiled.

With Tony Bedsoe dead, she felt there was nothing more for her to discover by working at the Blue Onion. It was time for her to make a change.

CHAPTER SEVENTEEN

TOYS FOR TOTS

Nicole stepped from the shower, looked in the mirror above the vanity, and was pleased to see that her face was still unblemished by age. She stood there wondering if she had made a wise decision by going to work at the Two O'Clock Club. It was a much higher class club and she doubted if she would find the person responsible for her daughter's murder hanging out there. But there was still the after-hour clubs to consider, and they were open all night. The Wee Hours would most likely be her best bet for continuing her search. It was always 'poppin' and she looked forward to seeing the owner, Gus. He made her laugh.

Next, she thought about Bulldog and how he was responsible for putting the Toys for Tots run together. The run would start in Baltimore, go to Hagerstown, then up through Annapolis and finally back to Baltimore. It was supposed to be a one hundred mile run, which was estimated by looking at a map. It was the one time a year that bikers from other clubs rode together as brothers. Everyone wore their colors proudly, the ride honoring fallen members and to help care for children who were less fortunate during Christmas time. It was something that seemed to warm Bulldog's heart, and made her like him even more. He had explained to her that there would be no fights, the penalty for fighting with a rival biker was very severe.

Bulldog had promised to pick her up at her apartment around ten o'clock that morning and it was already nine. She walked naked from the bathroom to her bedroom and into the walk-in closet and grabbed a pair of worn jeans and a small white halter top. She quickly dressed, looked in the mirror and saw her belly button clearly exposed. She thought she looked sexy, the feeling of not wearing underwear and riding bitch behind Bulldog excited her. As Peaches browsed through her purse she saw the business card the governor had given her. She pulled it out of her purse and read what was written on the back. There was a private phone number on the back and the words, "Call me anytime between nine a.m. and three p.m." Peaches picked up the phone on the night-stand next to her bed and dialed the number.

"Hello?"

"Is this Governor Marvin Mandell?"

"Yes, it is. May I ask whose calling?"

"Peaches, you..."

"Oh! Hi Peaches. I enjoyed your performance. I was wondering if you would call."

"I'm surprised you remember me," she laughed.

"I was wondering if you did any private shows?"

"I never have, but what do have in mind?"

"A private show. Let's say, for about three hours."

"That would cost three hundred dollars an hour," Peaches replied flatly. Before now, she never given it a thought. The number just seemed to her to be the right amount.

"That's fine. What evenings are you available? From six to nine p.m. would be best for me."

"Would it be okay if I call you back tomorrow? I'm not sure what my days off are going to be."

"That would be fine. Please call me, Marvin."

"Okay. Marvin, it is." Nicole smiled to herself, then she heard the roar of motorcycles outside. "I've got to go! I'm going on a Toys for Tots run. Would you like to make a donation," she said quickly.

"Of course! Tell the sponsors that I will be donating five hundred dollars."

"I'm sure the boys will be happy to hear that, governor. Thank you!"

"Peaches," he laughed. "Please call me Marvin."

"Okay, Marvin." Hearing a knock on the apartment door, she hurriedly said her goodbyes, hung up the phone, and rushed to answer the door.

"Hi." She smiled broadly, while wrapping both arms around Bulldog's neck.

He grabbed her around the waist, picked her up and hugged her close. As her tiny feet left the floor she bent her legs, trusting him to hold her up.

"How have you been? Did you miss me," he grinned.

"Of course I did. By the way, Governor Marvin Mandell is making a donation of five hundred dollars to the Toys for Tots fund."

"The governor?" Bulldog chuckled. "You are full of surprises."

A few minutes later when they stepped out of the apartment building Nicole saw a long line of parked motorcycles running from one end of the parking lot to the other. There were at least a hundred or more Argots present in the group. Bulldog quickly escorted her over to a bearded man in his mid to late thirties. She looked at him with an appraising eye. He had shoulder length brown hair, brown eyes, and his chiseled features were that of experience and wisdom. He was six feet tall and one hundred and ninety pounds of wiry muscle.

"Peaches, this is our club president, Ramrod. Ramrod, Peaches."

Peaches and Ramrod looked at each other and nodded their heads acknowledging each other. She sensed immediately that he was not the kind of man to trifle with. Bulldog opened a saddlebag on his bike and handed her a jacket, marking Peaches as his property. She looked at the name on the upper left corner of the leather. Where it had once been blank, it now read 'Peaches'.

"Does this make me your old lady," she asked.

"I guess it does." Bulldog grinned.

"Then don't let me catch any other tramp sitting on my bitch seat," she ordered.

Those close enough to hear her words laughed. Ramrod gave no more than a grin.

"We'll talk later." Bulldog sighed, quickly changing the subject by announcing, "Thanks to Peaches the governor is donating five hundred dollars to the Toys for Tots fund."

"He's got my vote." Ramrod said. Everyone knew that a vote from him was a vote from the club.

The bikers cranked their engines and they roared off into traffic and the sun filled day. Other clubs joined in along the route. Before the end of the run there were well over five hundred motorcycles completing the train of bikers and their women.

* * *

After the run was over and they were back in the city, Peaches, Bulldog and Ramrod returned to her apartment to talk business. They were seated around her kitchen table, the two men drinking bottles of Budweiser. Budweiser was a favored beer among the bikers. Ramrod started the conversation by saying, "I hear you have a steady connect ion for kilos of cocaine?"

"For twenty-eight thousand a kilo I'll supply all that you can handle."

"I bet you would." Ramrod chuckled. "Do you have a sample?"

Peaches went to her bedroom, grabbed her stash of cocaine, then returned to the kitchen offering an eighth of an ounce to Ramrod. He immediately laid out six lines, two for each of them, and offered a rolled up dollar bill to Peaches. She snorted a line into each nostril, tilted her head back, and sniffed hard. Then, Bulldog and Ramrod took their turns. They sat riding the high of the powerful cocaine for five minutes. Ramrod countered her price with an offer of twenty-five thousand a kilo, adding that he'd take ten kilos to start with.

"Cash on delivery?" Peaches asked.

"C.O.D. I will send someone to pick them up at your apartment."

"When?"

"The day after tomorrow works for me. Expect someone between three and four o'clock in the afternoon. Don't screw me over, little girl." Ramrod warned.

The second that Ramrod and Bulldog left the apartment, Nicole picked up the phone and called Charlie. After five rings, he answered. "Hello."

"We need to talk, now," she pressed.

"Where do you want to meet?"

"Somewhere halfway between my place and yours."

"The Truck Stop. I can't remember the name of it. Take the first exit after you go through the harbor tunnel and it's a half mile down on the right."

"I'll meet you there in forty-five minutes."

* * *

When Charlie arrived an hour later at the Truck Stop, Nicole's Mercedes was parked at the entrance of the restaurant. She was sitting in a booth at the rear of the eatery. Two truckers sat at a linoleum counter eating a breakfast meal, otherwise the place was empty of customers. As Charlie sat down, she smiled and proudly announced. "I've made a deal to sell ten kilos of cocaine," she spoke quietly.

"What's the deal?" Charlie grinned.

"I'm selling ten kilos tomorrow for twenty-five thousand dollars each. I'm taking two thousand dollars a kilo for myself for putting the deal together and taking the risks."

"What happened to the twenty-eight thousand dollars a kilo? Do you think I'm nuts? Do you think I'm going to settle for a measly five thousand dollars a kilo for myself!"

"Do I think you're nuts? You stupid asshole," she leaned forward to hiss at him. "I'm making you fifty thousand dollars cash. By the end of a month, that's two hundred thousand dollars. In five months you will be a fuckin' millionaire. You tell me if you're nuts, Charlie? You are an ungrateful arrogant asshole."

"Take it easy, baby. I didn't think about it like that. When do you want the kilos?"

"I want them at my apartment by noon tomorrow. I will personally bring you the cash as soon as the deal is finished."

"Maybe we can have a little fun when I bring you the cocaine,"

Charlie smiled.

"This is strictly business. Don't ever drop by my place unannounced. You may get your feelings hurt."

"Oh, so you do have a boyfriend. Is it that cop?"

"No!" Nicole said. "It's nunya," she laughed.

"Nunya?" Charlie mimicked her.

"Nunya damn business, Charlie."

* * *

It was Sunday night, and the Two O'Clock Club was very busy when Nicole stopped by. Once again Blaze was at her place at the bar, her flaming red hair making her easy to spot.

"Hi, Blaze." Peaches smiled. "I just stopped by to find out what nights I'm going to work."

"I'd like for you to work Sunday through Thursday night. Sunday, Monday, and Tuesday nights have been traditionally slow. I'm hoping you're working those nights will help boost my business. Did I explain the tips are collected by the bartender and split equally between the girls weekly. Everybody makes the same amount unless you take a night off. If you do, you will lose your portion of the tips for the entire week along with a day's pay. I pay weekly. Fifteen hundred dollars a week plus tips in cash on Friday night. The tips are generally another three hundred dollars."

Peaches and Blaze talked until closing.

* * *

After leaving the Two O'Clock Club Nicole drove to the Wee Hours, parked her silver Mercedes-Benz convertible behind Gus' red 1965 Chevrolet Malibu Super Sport convertible, put the top up, set the alarm, and asked the doorman to keep an eye on her car. He promised he would.

As she walked inside the after-hour club she saw Gus in the back talking to Jerry Everhart. Weaving her way through the tables and chairs, she stepped closer to the two men and overheard Jerry speaking softly, so not to be overheard.

"The last place Missy was seen alive was here at the Wee Hours," she heard Jerry say.

Peaches moved a few feet over to the bar, but still within hearing distance of their conversation. Jerry was noticeably upset, talking louder than normal, and Gus was trying to calm him down by talking softly.

"If I knew anything, I would tell you!" Gus swore loyalty to the other man. They had been friends for a lot of years.

"The detective told me there was semen and blood in her ass and Missy had two broken fingernails which indicates she put up a fight."

"That's fucked up," Gus retorted, then added with a thoughtful look on his face. "I don't know how Missy would have got in the door. I barred her for life because I caught her with heroin in her purse. She had several syringes too."

"All I know is the detective told me that the Wee Hours is the last place Missy was seen alive."

Instinctively, Gus glanced towards the bar. He saw Peaches standing there and quickly ushered Jerry into his office at the rear of the bar, and closed the door.

"A few days after the body was found in the harbor, Domonic came into the club. I remember he had a band-aid on his face. When I asked him what happened, he told me he cut himself shaving."

"Oh yeah!" Jerry snarled.

"This is between us, right?" Gus asked, almost pleading.

"Of course! Anything you tell me is strictly between us."

"Missy led a hard life but no one deserved what happened to her," Gus said, thinking about the crabs eating away half of her face.

Out in the club, Peaches was at the bar waiting for Jerry and Gus to reappear.

"Want something to drink," The barmaid Rose asked Peaches. "Just a coke." Peaches smiled handing Rose a dollar.

When Gus and Jerry walked out of the office they immediately saw Peaches sitting at the bar. Jerry smiled at the sight of her standing at the counter.

"Traitor," he teased. Peaches laughed.

"Don't be hassling my customers," Gus grinned.

"Nobody has danced on the stripper pole since you and Stormy," Jerry frowned.

"She danced for you?" Gus smiled his approval.

"That's not all I did for him," Peaches giggled.

"Oh, now we've got secrets," Gus retorted.

Jerry shrugged his shoulders. "It's not a secret, the girls love me!" Jerry grinned and started laughing.

CHAPTER EIGHTEEN

JINGLE BELLS

At precisely eleven forty-five a.m. Charlie knocked on the door of Nicole's apartment. She looked through the peephole, opened the door, and smiled when she saw the blue nylon gym bag in his right hand.

"Nice place." Charlie said with a smile, as he stepped inside. He immediately spotted the black leather Argot jacket hanging on the back of a kitchen chair with the name 'Peaches' on it. But what raised his eyebrows were the words 'Property of Bulldog'. "Who's Bulldog?" Charlie asked, grinning.

"Nunya, Charlie." Nicole laughed.

Charlie stacked the kilos on top of the kitchen table. They were individually wrapped in beige plastic. "You were wrong, that's two hundred and fifty thousand dollars."

"Wrong about what?"

"You said you would make me a millionaire in five months. It's four!" Charlie grinned. "When can I expect the money?"

"The deal will happen tomorrow afternoon. I will bring you the cash before I go to work tomorrow night."

"Work?" Charlie grinned.

"I have a job," Nicole admitted. She had not intended to tell him, but the cat was now out of the bag.

"Mind if I ask where you work?"

"Yes, I do. Mind your own business, Charlie."

"Wanna get lucky," he asked grinning.

"Do you have an eighth of an ounce?"

"You're a real bitch, Nicole."

"So what, you're an asshole. When you had this pussy for free you didn't want it. Now it's going to cost you every time!"

"It was never free," Charlie countered.

"Then why are you complaining?" Nicole asked smiling. "You're making twenty thousand dollars off me today. Isn't that enough?"

"The way I see it, I'm making you fifty thousand dollars." Nicole laughed as Charlie left the apartment.

* * *

Nicole picked up the phone and dialed Governor Marvin Mandell's number. After five rings he answered, 'Hello?"

"Hi Marvin, how are things with you this afternoon?"

"Just Peachy. How about you?"

"I'm good. I just wanted to call and let you know that my work hours are from nine p.m. until two a.m. Sunday through Thursday."

"How about if we get together Monday at the Hilton Hotel downtown around four p.m.?"

"That's fine. I will be in room 715. It's reserved."

"When we meet can I pick up a check for the five hundred dollar donation for the Toys for Tots fund?"

"Certainly. I will have a business check for that."

"I prefer cash for myself."

"No problem."

"Anything in particular you want me to wear?"

"Surprise me!"

"Okay," she giggled.

* * *

Bulldog and Ramrod were sitting in the cabin nursing hangovers from their night of heavy drinking when Bulldog asked, "Did you get in touch with the suit?"

"Everything is all set. He will be at Peaches apartment by three o'clock tomorrow afternoon. How well do you know this bitch?"

"Well enough to know she's crazy as hell!" Bulldog spoke seriously.

"But is she solid? Can she be trusted?"

"I would rather have her watch my back than most men. Do I trust her? When it comes to bitches I really think she's the best of the bunch. I feel pretty confident that she's not feeding us a line of bullshit."

"Good enough. I talked with some of the other club presidents during the toy run. I offered them kilos for twenty five thousand each."

"That's what we're paying for them," Bulldog snapped.

"Yes, but ours are uncut," Ramrod grinned. "Theirs will be cut and re-rocked."

"How do you re-rock powder cocaine?"

"With a trash compactor. I'll show you."

"Nothing surprises me anymore," Bulldog chuckled.

* * *

Three o' clock Thursday afternoon, Nicole heard a knock on the door of her apartment. She looked through the peephole expecting to see a biker. Instead, there was a man standing in front of the door wearing a suit and tie. Her first thought was that he was a detective. Nicole kept the chain on the door, opening it only partially.

"Can I help you," she asked.

"Peaches," he smiled.

"Yes."

"I believe we have some business to conduct. I'm here on behalf of Johnny Rowe."

"Johnny who," she asked not recognizing the name.

"You probably know him better as, Ramrod."

"Oh, I'm sorry," Nicole said, taking the chain off the door. You don't quite fit the picture of who I was expecting. I thought you were a detective!"

"Detectives don't generally wear three piece suits," he smiled pleasantly and introduced himself as attorney, Harold Glazer. In his right hand he carried a briefcase. He sat the briefcase on top of the kitchen table and opened it. It was packed with one hundred dollar bills. Two hundred and fifty thousand dollars in stacks of one thousand dollar wrappers. "You can count it if you like."

Nicole flipped through several bundles of the bills satisfying herself that there were no fake bills beneath the first bill. Then, she counted the stacks…all two hundred and fifty.

"You're welcome to count or test the kilos," Nicole smiled. "There are ten of them."

Harold Glazer smiled. Even though he was fifty pounds overweight, Nicole liked his wavy brown hair and rosy red cheeks.

"May I keep the gym bag," he asked.

"For two hundred and fifty thousand dollars I'll give you one every week," Nicole laughed escorting him to the door. She locked the door behind him and leaned back against it to take a much needed breath of release. During the entire transaction she had been nervous, needing things to desperately go as planned. Now that the first deal had gone as planned, she was certain Ramrod would trust her more in the future. Wearing a smile of pleasure, she went to go count out twenty thousand dollars for herself and put the rest in a shopping bag for Charlie.

She laid out double lines of cocaine and sniffed them hard into her left and right nostril. Feeling a nice buzz, she took time to wash the dishes in the kitchen sink, and take a shower before calling Charlie.

"I'll be to see you shortly," she said without preamble.

"See you then, babe."

Almost overnight the weather had gone from warm to cold, forcing Nicole to dress warmly before leaving the apartment, making sure she put on a warm jacket. It was the way of Baltimore weather, going from warm to cold in the blink of an eye. Soon it would be snow on the ground and boots and heavy coats would be the every day wear.

When she arrived at Charlie's one-story house a couple hours later, he was standing outside the front door, dressed warmly in a long leather coat. Nicole walked briskly past him into the house, going directly into the spacious kitchen. She dumped the money on top of the wooden kitchen table. "You can count it if you want. It's all in hundred dollar bills and it's all there."

Charlie laughed and grabbed her to swing her around in the air. "You're beautiful!"

"Am I still a bitch," she demanded, laughing along with him.

"That's hereditary babe," he said, still smiling. "But by the same token, I'm an asshole. It doesn't mean I don't love you."

"You love me?" Nicole said in surprise.

"In my own way. I just don't want any commitments."

"Neither do I." Nicole admitted.

"Then we do have something in common," Charlie grinned.

A few weeks later when Nicole went to Marsha's house, she found the door already unlocked, so she walked inside. The Christmas tree was lit up with presents thoughtfully placed beneath it. Marsha was sitting at the kitchen table wiping away tears.

"What's wrong?" Nicole asked in concern.

"This is our first Christmas without Harold and it just doesn't seem like Christmas."

Nicole understood how she felt. It would be her first Christmas without Charlotte. She did not know what to say, so she decided to redirect her friend's attention.

"I brought gifts for the kids and one for you and Manny," Nicole smiled.

"Thank you." Marsha smiled, wiping away her tears.

"Are we going to see Manny?"

"We go every Wednesday afternoon. He will be expecting us!" Marsha replied, continuing to force a smile.

"A few weeks ago when I went to the Wee Hours, Jerry Everhart, the owner of Hectors which is another after-hour club, was talking to Gus about a murder. Some girl named Missy was found murdered in the harbor. I think she worked as a prostitute for the Everhart brothers because Jerry was really pissed off."

"Why didn't you tell me about this sooner."

"It slipped my mind."

"Okay, but why is this so important?"

"I'm not sure. I just have this feeling that it does."

The two women sat there in silence, thinking about what the new information could possibly mean.

* * *

As the girls prepared to leave the house, Marsha suggested that she drive her car. Walking out the door, they both carried a Christmas present for Manny. Nicole tuned in the radio and sang along to the song playing while Marsha smiled and felt very much alone with her thoughts. Marsha parked beneath a light pole near the front door of the building where Manny's condo was, making it a short walk to the elevator. They rode the elevator to his floor, and knocked on the door to his condo.

"Ho, ho, ho…" Manny grinned as he opened the door inviting them inside. He was dressed in a Santa Claus outfit. Marsha and Nicole cracked up laughing.

"Merry Christmas!" Manny said. The dining room table was set for three and there was a turkey with all of the trimmings on the table.

"I thought tonight we would just enjoy each other's company," Manny grinned.

"You're the best!" Marsha smiled, giving him a big hug.

"I love you, Manny." Nicole declared, throwing her arms around his neck and making him blush his pleasure.

"There's gifts for you girls beneath the tree."

"I've been good," Nicole giggled. "So it better not be any switches. If it is I will use them on you."

Marsha hurried over to the Christmas tree wanting to be the first one to open her gift. She tore open the colorfully wrapped package like a little girl. "Oh, I've been a very good girl," she exclaimed, admiring a pair of one carat diamond earrings.

As Nicole opened her first present she announced, "I've been better than you," she admired her diamond tennis bracelet.

Manny had brought them both matching sets. The diamonds were large and clearly very expensive.

"And we have something special for you," Nicole smiled proudly, presenting her gift.

Manny opened her present for him. It was a gold Rolex watch with 'Love Nicole' engraved on the inside bezel.

"I can't top that." Marsha sighed, and handed Manny a present from her. It was two dozen homemade Christmas cookies.

"Thank you, so much." Manny said with tears in his eyes. He hugged them, one under each arm. "Now, let's eat."

Manny pulled the chairs back seating Marsha, then Nicole. He sat one on each side of him with himself at the head of the table. Nicole spoke first asking. "Would it be alright if I said grace?"

"Sure." Manny smiled his approval.

Nicole began. "Lord, thank you for this dinner. Thank you for giving me friends like Marsha, and Manny. Please help them through troubled times. Offer your guidance, wisdom, and understanding. And Lord, please look after Charlotte. Remind her every day of how much I love and miss her. In Jesus' name I pray. Amen."

"Amen." Marsha and Manny said in unison.

"Who is Charlotte?" Manny asked, reaching for the mashed potatoes. "Help yourselves," he urged.

"Charlotte was my daughter." Nicole spoke softly, wondering how much trust she should put in Manny. "She was only six years old when she was killed by a hit and run driver. The police labeled it an accident. But, to me, it was murder!" Nicole could not stop the tears that formed in her eyes. As a tear fell, Manny reached to wipe it away.

"Manny. You do know that Marsha and I both love you. You do know that, don't you," she whispered.

"I love you girls as well. You know that too, don't you?"

Manny grinned. "If either of you ever need someone to talk to, a place to stay, anything whatsoever. And I do mean anything. Call me or stop by. My door is always open to you."

"Aren't you hot in that outfit?" Marsha laughed while holding back tears of happiness.

Manny chuckled. "I am having a great difficulty eating," he pulled at the white beard.

"Why don't you put on something more comfortable?" Nicole suggested.

Manny took her advice and walked to his bedroom, returning wearing his white robe and his new Rolex watch. Manny looked at the gold watch and scolded Nicole, "You shouldn't have ..."

"Do you like it," she cut him off.

"I love it. It's the nicest and probably the most expensive gift any-one has ever given me."

"Nothing is too good for you Manny," Nicole said, and she meant it. She would never have thought of giving Charlie such an expensive, indescribable gift. Bulldog either. There was a trust, a love that only she, Marsha, and Manny could understand. The most important thing was their feelings were mutual.

"I've got one more surprise for you girls."

"What's that?" Marsha giggled and looked across the table at Nicole.

Manny walked into the kitchen, opened the oven, and took out a fresh baked apple pie. He sliced it, then opened the refrigerator and grabbed a quart of vanilla ice cream from the freezer. He put one scoop of ice cream on top of each slice of pie and served the girls.

"I made it myself," Manny said proudly.

"You are full of surprises." Marsha smiled.

"This is delicious," Nicole said, after taking a bite.

"But that's not the surprise," Manny grinned. "The surprise is that I'm paying all expenses for Marsha's children and you and her to spend New Years in Hawaii."

"I've got five kids!" Marsha declared.

"No problem. How about you, Nicole?"

"I'm divorced. My only child was murdered."

"Well, do you girls want to go to Hawaii, or not?"

"I want to go!" Nicole announced excitedly.

Marsha had a condition. Only if Manny went too. "It's a date." Manny grinned.

As an afterthought, Nicole hoped that Bulldog had no plans for the two of them. She was unsure what to say if he did. Whatever she told him, she was certain that it would not be the truth.

"I need to know when we are leaving and returning. I just started a new job, and I have to give my employer some notice."

"A new job. Where are you working?"

Nicole wished she would learn to think before she talked. She never wanted to lie to Manny. "I'm performing at the Two O'Clock Club downtown."

"You're working for Blaze? Ann and I have been friends for thirty years. Just tell her that you are going to Hawaii with me and she won't be upset at all. I promise you that."

"You are full of surprises," Nicole laughed.

Manny called the airport. Their departing flight would leave at two fifteen p.m. on December 28th. They would return at seven p.m. on the 3rd of January. Manny made reservations at the Hilton Hotel which was right on the beach on the island of Honolulu.

* * *

After visiting Manny, Nicole dropped Marsha off at her house. Marsha was excited and anxious to tell the kids they were all going to Hawaii, knowing it would do a lot to boost their spirit in the absence of their father. Since the murder of their dad, their little hearts had been filled with sadness.

When Nicole went to work, the first thing on her agenda was to ask Blaze if she knew Manny.

Blaze's eyes lit up. "Of course I know Manny!"

"Good, I need some time off work because he wants me to go to Hawaii with him from December 28th through the 3rd of January. He said that if I told you it was for him it would be all right."

"He's pulling the friendship card," Blaze laughed. "Manny knows I adore him and would never tell him no."

"Does that mean I can go?"

"Yes." Blaze said, tipping her drink and finishing it off. She sat the glass down on top of the bar counter and the bartender instantly refilled it.

Nicole was in a zone, the happiest she had been in a very long time and that night she gave the best performance ever.

CHAPTER NINETEEN
OFF LIMITS

Nicole was at home and just stepping out of the shower when she heard the telephone ring. She grabbed a towel from its rack and quickly tried to dry herself off as she ran naked for the bedroom. She sat down on the edge of the bed, snatched up the receiver, and said, "Hello?"

"Are you up?" Stormy's cheerful voice came over the line. "I'm surprised you're at home. I've been trying to get in touch with you for nearly a week."

"Hi Stormy." Nicole responded, finishing drying herself off. "Things have been pretty hectic lately."

"How are things going at work?"

"So far, great. I'm off on Friday and Saturday night."

"I've got a new gig. I'm dancing at the Body Shop. It's at eighteen thirteen West Pratt Street. It's a Saturday night. What do you have planned?"

"Nothing yet. I've been expecting Bulldog to call. I just got out of the shower and I'm sitting here naked freezing my ass off!"

"If you're not doing anything, drop by the bar. Don't let the appearance of the place scare you away," Stormy laughed.

"If I don't have a date I'll be there," Nicole promised.

Nicole dressed, blow dried her hair, and changed the linen on her bed before making a pot of coffee and sitting down at the kitchen table.

Twenty minutes later Bulldog called. "Hi baby. Did you find out what your off days are going to be?"

"I'm off tonight and tomorrow. Every Saturday and Sunday."

"It would be better for me if you had weekdays off," he replied, then added. "Thursday we are going to need another bunch of roses. Expect a visit between three and four."

"That's good to hear. Peanut will be happy to hear that. Before I forget to tell you, I'm going to be out of town from December twenty-eighth through January second. I'll be back on the third."

"How in the fuck are we supposed to take care of business if you're out of town. And while we're at it, who in the fuck is Peanut and where are you going?"

"Nunya," Peaches giggled.

"Nunya?" Bulldog growled, "What in the fuck does that mean?"

"None of your business," she laughed.

"Everything you do is my business. You are my property, Darlin'."

"You don't fuckin' own me. You can't tell me what I can or can't do! I have a mind of my own," she snapped.

"Is that right?"

"It's a fact, Jack."

"Let me catch you going anywhere not wearing your colors and I'll show you whose the boss."

"Is that right?"

"You can take that to the friggin' bank!"

"What will you do?"

"I'll be making myself a lot of friends because I'll pass your little ass around like a blind man passes a hat."

"You wouldn't do that to me."

"Try me."

"I might like it," Peaches giggled.

"Fuckin' bitch!" Bulldog growled and hung up the phone. Nicole laughed out loud.

* * *

Nicole called Charlie and told him she needed to speak with him in person. They agreed to meet at the Truck Stop in two hours. Charlie arrived before Nicole and parked his Corvette at the front of the restaurant. When Nicole arrived, she parked her Mercedes next to his car.

"What's up?" Charlie asked as she seated herself in the booth across from him. He took a sip of coffee and repeated the question, "What's up?"

"Why does it always have to be 'What's up'? Why can't you ask how I'm doing or offer me something to drink?"

"How are you? Would you care for something to drink? What's up? How's that?" Charlie grinned.

"Fuck you, asshole."

"That's the best offer I've had all week."

"May I take your order?" the elderly waitress asked Nicole.

"Coffee, please."

"Charlie," Nicole spoke quietly. "I need ten kilos tomorrow afternoon. Just like before! But there's a problem."

"What's that?"

"I'm going away on vacation from December twenty-eighth and returning on January third. The Argots are really upset about that. What I need from you is when they come for the ten kilos, front them an additional ten. It's just good business!"

"Are you nuts? You want me to front a quarter million dollars worth of cocaine? That's insane!"

"Fuck you! I'm getting real sick of people telling me I'm nuts. What's insane is that someone fronted you five times that amount and you have no way of selling it by yourself. That's really insane, Charlie. The Argots are about their business. Don't fuck this deal up!"

"What the fuck. A blind man can't see and a scared man shouldn't gamble. I'll see you around Two O'Clock tomorrow afternoon, babe."

"Thanks Charlie," Nicole smiled. She took a sip of hot coffee, stood up, and walked out of the restaurant.

It was a cold and freezing day, with dark clouds in the sky and light flurries of snow in the air. A flock of geese flew overhead, making a late start South for the winter. In just a few more days she would also be heading for a warmer climate, flying away in another direction. She could hardly wait to sun her buns on the beaches of Honolulu.

After leaving Charlie at the Truck Stop, Nicole drove to the Harrendale Mall in Glen Burnie and went shopping. She purchased several pair of shorts, a new swim suit, Levi's, two halter tops, and a pair of flip-flops. She bought Bulldog a ring for Christmas. It was 14k gold, with a cluster of diamonds in the shape of a horseshoe. She hoped he would like it. It was Christmas Eve and she had no plans. Nicole wondered what Charlie, Marsha, Manny, and Bulldog were doing. Bulldog should have made plans to be with her, she thought. As quickly as she had thought that, she reasoned that she had made no plans to be with him on New Years Eve. It was like the pot calling the kettle black! Stormy had invited her to the Body Shop. It was time to stop by and surprise her, and maybe the two of them would make the circuit after closing.

Nicole stopped at a flower shop and purchased the nicest wreath they had. Then, she drove to the cemetery where Charlotte was buried. Disregarding the frozen weather, she stooped down to pick the shriveled weeds from around Charlotte's headstone. When she was finished, she lay the reef against the headstone, then got down on her knees to pray. Her headstone was a shiny gray granite with Charlotte's full name, date of birth, and the date of her death skillfully engraved. Nicole wept as she prayed to God for forgiveness of her sins and asked that Charlotte be blessed with his mercy. She slowly stood up, walked back to the Mercedes and keyed the ignition.

Arriving back at the apartment Nicole parked in the underground garage, covered the Mercedes with its protective cover and set the alarm. Tonight she would drive her beloved yellow bug, over a week having passed since she had last driven it; her fondness for the car not allowing her to go too long without taking it out for a drive. It reminded her of her modest roots, and sometimes she could visualize Charlotte sitting in the front seat beside her. Those wonderful memories made her promise herself that she would never part with the Volkswagon.

Nicole dressed and as an after thought grabbed her leather jacket.

Wearing her colors was a sign of respect for her old man, Bulldog. If she was wearing it and anyone disrespected her they were disrespecting him. It would not be tolerated by any member of the club.

Nicole put on her jacket and left the apartment. It was nine o'clock in the evening. She parked the yellow Bug at the curb of the Body Shop. She heard gunshots, two of them back to back. Bang ... bang. A young black male ran past her with several other young blacks in pursuit. One of them held a small caliber pistol in his right hand and he had it pointed straight out in front of him. As they ran out of sight Nicole opened the car door, then hurried down the sidewalk for half a block to the Clubs front entrance. When she entered the club, Stormy was there waiting for her with the club's owner.

"I heard the gunshots," Stormy said, the relief plain on her face.

"I'm fine!" Nicole assured her with a smile.

"Well, Merry Christmas!" Stormy hugged her affectionately.

"This is Chris Howden, he's the owner. He just moved here from Michigan two years ago. Some of the girls call him T & T. Like dynamite, he's sometimes quick to explode."

"My boyfriend has that problem," Nicole laughed.

"I don't have that problem!" Chris protested loudly, drawing the attention of the other patrons to the front entrance. "The pleasure is not all mine," he grinned, placing emphasis on the not.

Stormy and Peaches looked at each other then burst into laughter. Chris was well dressed in black Hagger slacks, a white Polo shirt, and polished black leather loafers. His shirt was opened slightly showing off a thick gold chain. As Nicole looked around she noticed that the club was a mixture of whites, blacks, and Mexicans. The inside was tastefully decorated, more so than the Blue Onion. Chris did not care what nationality someone claimed, as long as their money was green and they respected his club, the door was always open to them.

"I see Bulldog has claimed you as his property," Stormy smiled.

"Nobody owns me!" Nicole countered, in a serious tone.

"Can I get you something to drink?" Chris offered.

"Thank you. I'll have a Long Island Iced-Tea."

"Good choice." Stormy smiled, remembering that Nicole was not much of a drinker.

"There's a stripper pole here." Stormy pointed to the stage in the far corner of the bar. "You should see this girl perform, Chris."

"I'd love to," he replied, grinning.

"What's up with the black guys chasing and shooting at each other. Is it always like that?"

"Naw. That's just some young punks running away their competition. This street belongs to the Pratt Street Boys. If someone tries to sell drugs on their turf, there's going to be fireworks. If they were serious about shooting the guy, you would have heard a lot more than just two shots."

"Two was enough for me, especially when I don't have a gun."

Chris and Stormy laughed, After drinking two Long Island Iced Tea's, Stormy talked Peaches into pole dancing. Peaches handed Chris her jacket with instructions for him to protect it with his life. She danced seductively across the room to the pole, several people moving out of her way to let her pass by. She grabbed the pole with one hand while thrusting her pelvis slowly back and forth, humping the pole with pretended passion. All eyes were on her, including Chris. There was not a limp dick in the bar. Peaches was dancing provocatively. Nasty in a sexy kind of way. Chris loved her performance and offered her a job the second she reached them through the applause of the room.

"The tips are excellent," Stormy added.

After three more Long Island Iced Tea's, Peaches begin to slur her words badly. "After closing, let's go to the Weeeee Hours."

"I'll follow you," Stormy laughed. If Peaches was going to run into someone, Stormy did not want it to be her.

When the club closed, they made their way to the Wee Hours. Peaches parked the yellow Bug behind a white Cadillac. As she locked the car, she looked across the street and watched Stormy park. Peaches hugged herself against the cold, the small biker leather not enough to keep her warm for long.

Domonic Coroza walked out of the Wee Hours. When he saw Peaches he recognized her immediately and said, "Let me talk to you for a minute." He opened the passenger door of his Cadillac parked at the curb and motioned for her to have a seat. Stormy crossed the street and stopped at the rear of the Cadillac. "Is everything alright, Peaches," she questioned, going pale at the sight of Domonic.

"It's cool." Nicole replied, then climbed into the passenger seat.

Domonic barely gave Stormy a glance as he went around to slide behind the steering wheel of the Cadillac. "It's nice to see you."

"It's nice to see you to ... o ... o" Peaches smiled, slurring her words slightly.

"I'm sorry to hear about Tony," Domonic lied.

"It's sad." Peaches admitted, then offered. "I'm working at the Two O'Clock Club now."

"That's a nice club," Domonic replied. "My friend's birthday is the second of January, and I would like to hire you to dance at his party."

"I'm going to be in Hawaii. Did you ask Stormy? She might be available, but we don't take our shoes off for less than three hundred dollars an hour."

Domonic used the power button to roll down the passenger side window and motioned for Stormy to join them inside the Cadillac. He explained what he wanted. Stormy hesitated for a minute before accepting.

"His name is Jimmy Edwards," Domonic said, passing one of Jimmy's business cards to Stormy, "That's his home address on the card, and here's your money." Domonic handed Stormy three crisp One Hundred dollar bills.

"Thanks for the business," Stormy smiled, shoving the money into her purse.

Peaches and Stormy climbed out of the car and watched as Domonic drove away. As they began to enter the after-hour club, Stormy froze in her tracks.

"Shit," she cursed.

"What?" Peaches asked, standing beside her.

"I'm not going to be able to keep that appointment. I'm going to be at a family reunion in Kentucky. Domonic is going to be furious."

"Oh well," Peaches laughed. "He'll get over it."

After completing the circuit of the after-hour clubs, the girl's parted company and went home.

The following day there was a knock on Nicole's apartment door around noon. She struggled to get out of bed and walked down the short hallway wearing a large T-shirt. She looked through the peephole, then opened the door for Charlie, who was busy brushing snow off of his long overcoat.

"It looks like one of us had fun last night," Charlie chuckled, closing the door behind him.

"All I got was drunk," she replied. She sat down in a chair at the dinning room table, curling one small foot under her ass, and cupping her head in her hands.

Without any more small talk, Charlie sat a blue gym bag on the table. It contained twenty kilos of pure cocaine. Nicole promised to bring him two hundred and fifty thousand dollars in cash before she went to work Monday night. Tuesday afternoon she would be on a flight to Honolulu.

Nicole's head was splitting and she was not looking forward to going to work that evening. Monday her schedule was going to be crazy. Deliver the drugs, dance for the governor, and meet Charlie before she went to work. It was too much to think about at the moment, so she went back to bed.

At five o'clock in the afternoon, Nicole finally crawled out of the bed. She took a cold shower, swallowed four aspirins, and dressed warmly in wool slacks flared at the bottom and a sweater. She walked into the kitchen, opened the refrigerator, grabbed a carton of orange juice and poured herself a glass. She toasted two slices of bread. The thought of buttering the toast was nauseating, so she ate it plain.

At eight forty-five she parked her Mercedes-Benz in front of the Two O'Clock Club and reported for work. It was midnight when the roar of Harley's penetrated the walls of the club. One by one the bikers rolled their Harley's backwards parking the rear wheels against the curb. Ramrod and Bulldog led a pack of bearded bikers into the club, ignoring the sign at the front door which read 'No Club Colors.' When the bouncer attempted to enforce the rule, Bulldog asked how he felt about eating his meals through a straw for the next few months. The bouncer stepped aside.

Peaches was sitting at the bar on a stool next to Blaze, the relationship they shared with Manny having brought them closer together. Bulldog and Ramrod bellied up to the bar with a dozen of their brothers. Peaches excused herself and walked over to talk with Bulldog.

"I'll be right back," she told him, rushing off to the girls dressing room. When she returned, she placed the 14k gold diamond horseshoe ring on Bulldog's right index finger.

He smiled approvingly, giving her a long passionate kiss. "Who's your daddy," he asked grinning.

"You are! But you can't be coming in here like this."

"Like what," he laughed.

Nicole decided to soften him up before demanding what she wanted. "I've got another surprise for you. When Harold brings the money for the ten roses, I will give him another ten roses on commission," she spoke in code just in case someone other than Ramrod, was listening.

"Why didn't you tell me this sooner. I thought you were leaving me with a problem, so I was bringing one to your doorstep."

"I would never intentionally do that to you. Before I could tell you I needed to get approval from Peanut."

"Who is Peanut?"

"My connect."

"Where are you going?"

"My grandmother is dying of Leukemia. I'm going to visit her." Well, Nicole thought, a girl can't be honest about everything. She laughed silently to herself.

"Okay." Bulldog grunted.

"From now on, the Two O'Clock Club is off limits to Argots."

"No place is off limits to me." Bulldog declared.

"Wanna bet?" Peaches snickered, then turned to Ramrod. "Ramrod, if we are going to continue doing business I need you to back me up on this one."

"It's off limits!" Ramrod grinned, but there was no humor in his eyes.

"You're a fuckin' bitch!" Once again she had bested him. The bikers downed their drinks and quietly left the bar. Nicole rejoined Blaze.

"If that happens again, I don't want to, but I'll have to let you go," Blaze sighed.

Peaches smiled broadly and replied, "It won't happen again!"

CHAPTER TWENTY
HONOLULU BABY

Manny called Marsha and asked for the names, ages, and birth dates of her five children. Then he asked for her home address, explaining he would be sending a limousine to take her and the children to the airport. Marsha argued that it really was unnecessary, but Manny insisted that he understood the difficulty of her organizing for five children plus herself. He purchased eight first class tickets for himself, Marsha, Nicole and the five children.

* * *

Nicole awoke at nine o'clock in the morning feeling surprising well, considering the amount of alcohol she had consumed the night before. She showered, shaved her legs and armpits, then painted her finger and toenails a hot pink. She wrapped herself in a white robe, hung her black leather jacket in the hall closet, picked up any clutter around the house, then washed her dirty clothes. Peaches patiently took the time to pack her suitcase with shorts, jeans, two bikinis, two cocktail dresses, two pair of high-heels, and a pair of flip-flops.

On her bed, she laid out a short black leather skirt, a white blouse with ruffles, a black leather vest, and a pair of black stiletto high-heels. Under the leather skirt, she wore a black g-string. She thought Marvin would approve of her choice. From a jewelry box on top of her dresser she picked out a set of one carat diamond earrings with a matching diamond tennis bracelet that Manny had gifted her and carefully placed the selected jewelry on top of the dresser.

* * *

At precisely three p.m. the doorbell rang. Nicole looked through the peephole and she was pleased to see the Argots representative was on time. Quickly opening the door, she invited Harold Glazer inside with a huge smile.

"I don't mean to rush you, but I'm in a bit of a hurry."

"No problem," Harold grinned as he opened his briefcase and began placing stacks of one hundred dollar bills on top of the dining room table. "You do know this would be much easier it your people would except a Cashier's check. They are probably paying some banker points to exchange their money and I could give you a Cashier's check or send a wire transfer to the bank of their choice."

"I'll suggest that," Nicole promised. At the moment she was just trying to make it through the night. She had to meet with the governor at the Hilton Hotel downtown, then rush over to Charlie's house and give him the bag of money, and then finally go to work.

"Is the blue gym bag mine to keep?" Harold smiled pleasantly.

"Of course," Nicole said, returning the smile. "Only this time there's twenty kilos of cocaine in it, so it may be a little heavier to tote. You can count those if you want?"

"Did you count them," he asked.

"Yes, I did."

"That's good enough for me," Harold smiled. He picked up the gym bag and walked out the door.

* * *

Nicole took twenty thousand dollars from the table, placed it inside a shoe box with the steadily growing pile of money she was quickly accumulating. She hid the box on a shelf in the hall closet behind a number of other boxes. Next, she entered the kitchen and grabbed a brown shopping bag from a cupboard beneath the sink. Returning to the dining room and filled the bag with the money for Charlie.

After closing the bag she returned to the bedroom to put the diamond earrings carefully on her ears. She clasped the diamond bracelet around her left wrist before going to a mirror to admire herself. Assured that everything was in its rightful place, she grabbed her long overcoat and the bag of money from the dining room table and left the apartment. Alone in the underground garage she turned the alarm off the Mercedes-Benz and placed the bag of money in the trunk. She was soon speeding off to meet the governor at the Hilton Hotel downtown.

She parked the car and climbed out from behind the wheel, setting the alarm. From the moment she entered the lobby of the Hotel all eyes were on her. She approached the elevator and pressed the up button, very much aware of the eyes following her sexy walk. When the elevator arrived, she rode it alone up to the seventh floor. Nicole stepped out, looked at the numbers on the wall directly in front of the elevator and proceeded down the hall to the left. She stopped at room 715, ran her fingers through her platinum blonde hair, and knocked lightly on the door.

Governor Marvin Mandell looked through the peephole, opened the door and invited her inside with a broad smile. Two men dressed in suits were sitting in chairs watching a game of football on the television.

"I expected you to be by yourself," Nicole smiled.

"I am. These are my bodyguards and they were just leaving. isn't that right, guys?"

"I promise not to hurt him." Nicole teased.

"Just so you know, we have rooms on both sides," one of the state troopers announced, laughing. They closed the door as they left the room.

The Governor led her immediately into a plush bedroom. Nicole looked around the room. There was a king sized bed, two night stands with lamps, two plush chairs, a television, and a full bath. On a scale of one to ten, the decor was a solid ten. She peeked out of the curtains and the view of the city was spectacular.

"There's a five hundred dollar check made out to Toys for Tots on the table," Marvin pointed.

"Do you have any music you want me to dance to," she asked.

"Darlin', I think we both know I'm really not interested in watching you dance."

Nicole smiled.

"From the moment I saw you," Marvin continued, "I've thought of nothing more than making love to you."

"Wow! That's pretty much right to the point. There's no beating around the bush with you, is there?" Peaches traced her lips with her tongue, then added. "It's going to cost you! Six hundred dollars if you want the full Peaches pleasure package."

Marvin was throbbing with anticipation. He grabbed his wallet from his back pocket, counted out six hundred dollars and passed it to her with a shaky hand. As she accepted the money, he grabbed her to turn her around to kiss her on the neck, running his hand beneath her blouse, and gently squeezing her small, firm breasts. He rolled her nipples between his thumb and forefinger until they became rock hard. Marvin pressed his body against hers allowing her to feel his manhood as it grew larger and larger.

Peaches turned her head to the side and he kissed her passionately. Using his left hand he unbuttoned her blouse, while running his right hand down to the bottom of her inner thigh, slowly exploring her hidden treasures. He felt the g-string between her legs and then the warmth of her hot moist pussy. He massaged her clit, pulled her g-string to the side, and inserted a finger slowly inside her tightness. He hiked her skirt up, parted her legs, and told her to lean over the bed. He dropped his trousers and shorts in one quick motion, and entered her moist cunt from the rear. It was warm, tight, and inviting, everything he expected and more than he had imagined it to be. He thrust hard, burying his manhood to the hilt.

Nicole moaned in unexpected pleasure. He fucked her hard for a good five minutes, pulled out, threw her across the bed, and began ravishing her body with his tongue, while playing with her hard nipples. He twisted her around on the bed and kissed her from head to toe, then slowly and methodically began eating her pussy. Peaches sucked his dick as if it was her last meal, wanting him to remember her long after she had left. Before cumming he stopped her, turned her back around, and fucked her even harder than before. He grabbed her ankles, one in each hand, and held them high over her head. Peaches moaned in sheer ecstasy, almost overcome with pleasure. Marvin banged her hot pussy until he collapsed and laid next to her in exhaustion.

"My god, you've got my vote," she laughed.

Peaches felt no sense of guilt. Bulldog had left her alone for the holidays. If he had taken good care of her she would not have been so damn horny. Then she chuckled to herself. Who was she kidding? The governor was a good looking powerful man, and she would have fucked him for free just to get on his good side.

There was no conversation between the two of them. Marvin lay on the bed resting and watching Peaches as she dressed and prepared to leave. She sat down on the edge of the bed, leaned over, and kissed him goodbye.

"It's been fun," he smiled, as he watched her walk out of the room.

* * *

It was seven-thirty when Nicole pulled into Charlie's driveway. His Corvette was not present, which was not a good sign. She opened the trunk of the Mercedes, grabbed the grocery bag and knocked on the front door of his house. Within seconds she heard footsteps and Charlie answered the door.

"Where's your car," she asked immediately.

"I wrecked it. It's in the shop being repaired."

"How did you wreck it?"

"I was looking at a girl crossing the street in a mini-skirt and not paying attention. The car in front of me stopped and by the time I looked up and hit the brakes I was sliding right under his rear bumper. My right headlight and some fiberglass ended up on the ground. I was pissed off, but it was my fault. What more could I do?"

"Stop looking at girls while you're driving," Nicole suggested.

"You look hot! I love that outfit," Charlie grinned.

"I would love to stay and play but I have to be at work in a hour. By this time tomorrow you can be thinking about me bathing in the sun in Honolulu."

"Aloha," he said, as he began counting the money.

Nicole went to work, focusing all of her attention on her performance. After work she went directly home, she wanted to be well rested for her trip.

                                    * * *

At ten o'clock in the morning the following day Nicole rushed to the hair salon to have her hair professionally dyed platinum blonde. The beautician added a few highlights that looked really terrific.

The limousine arrived thirty minutes early to pick Marsha and the kids up. The driver wanted to make sure that there was plenty of time to load the luggage and get the children organized. Being a single mother with five kids, he knew it would not be an easy task for her.

Nicole decided to drive her Bug to the airport and leave it in long term parking for a week. She would ride the shuttle to the terminal.

Manny arrived before Nicole and they waited just inside the terminal for the limousine to arrive with Marsha and the kids. When the limousine pulled up to the curb, the kids jumped out like a band of wild Indians. They were excited and ready to go.

Marsha stepped out of the limousine, smiled, and said, "They are full of energy." Manny and Nicole laughed.

"Settle down!" Marsha yelled at the children once they were out of the cold and into the airport terminal. She began the introductions. "Children, this is my friend, Mr. Manny. Manny, this is my oldest son, Travis. He's twelve. This is my daughter Carla. She's eight." Marsha moved from one child to the next, placing her right hand on the top of their heads.

"These are my twins, Jimmy and Danny. They are six. My baby, Megan is five. We call Danny 'Freckles.' I'm sure you can understand why," Marsha smiled, patting him on top of his head of red hair. "I call Megan sunshine because she brightens up my day."

"Call me Uncle Manny," Manny suggested.

"Hi, Uncle Manny!" The children chorused.

"Well, we better get moving if we don't want to miss our flight," Manny grinned.

For the most part the children were well behaved. When spoken to they answered, "Yes, Sir, and yes, Ma'am."

"There's something different about you." Nicole declared, taking a closer look at Manny.

"It's the beard Nicole," Marsha smiled. He had grown a closely cut beard. It was gray, but quite distinguished looking. It looked so natural that Nicole had barely noticed it.

They checked their luggage, walked through the terminal, and boarded the airplane. After seating themselves, while waiting for the flight to take-off, Manny thought it would be a good time for him to get better acquainted with the children. He asked the oldest, Travis, "What do you want to be when you grow up?"

"A pilot," he answered quickly. "I want to fly the friendly skies and go wherever I want."

"How about you boys," he asked the twins.

"Jimmy grinned, showing a very lonely tooth, replied. "I want to be a fireman."

"What do you want to be, Freckles?"

"I want to be a carpenter and build huge skyscrapers."

"That's a pretty big goal. Are you working hard in school and getting good grades?"

"I'm trying." Danny said solemnly.

"How about you Carla?"

"I want to be a nurse," she answered flatly.

"What do you want to be when you grow up, Sunshine?"

Megan twisted her head back and forth, then shouted, "I want to be rich. Then I can go and do whatever I want!" Manny, Nicole, and Marsha laughed heartily.

"I see why you call her, Sunshine." Manny grinned.

"She always brightens my day." Marsha smiled.

"Ladies and gentlemen, this is your Captain speaking. We are preparing for take-off. Please make sure your overhead luggage is properly secured, buckle your seat-belts, and remain seated until the overhead light goes off. Thank you for flying American Airlines and we hope you have a pleasant flight."

Shortly after take-off Manny was bombarded with questions from the children. Where do you live? How old are you? What kind of work do you do? It was seven hours of Uncle Manny or Aunt Nicole, can I have this or will you do that? The questions were unending, but the bond between Manny and the children were slowly blooming. For him it felt good being a part of a larger family.

When the airplane landed in Honolulu a black stretch limousine was parked at the curb waiting to take them to the Hilton Hotel. The weather was beautiful, the sun shinning bright in the clear blue sky. They were greeted by Hula dancers and colorful leis were draped over their heads in welcome. This seemed to excite the children as much as the summer-like heat. Manny already had reservations for a three bedroom suite for Marsha and the children. Directly across the hall he rented adjacent rooms for himself and Nicole.

Manny and Nicole walked Marsha and the kids to their suite. The kids ran straight for the balcony, opened the glass sliding door, and stood outside looking down on the pristine beach. The beach was crowded with bright umbrellas, folding chairs, and people laying on towels and blankets sunbathing. In the ocean there were kids on rafts, surfers, and the view of the white sandy beach was endless. The leaves on the palm trees blew wildly in the wind. The scenery was picturesque, breathtaking and beautiful.

A maid wearing a brown apron was standing in the kitchen. She was a heavy set Hawaiian woman in her mid-forties, who looked very capable and sweet.

"Marsha, children," Manny announced. "This is Kiloa. She will be your nanny during your vacation in Hawaii. It is her job to help your mother look after you."

"You're amazing!" Marsha smiled, resisting the temptation to throw her arms around Manny's neck and kiss him. She did not want her kids to see that.

"Mr. Manny rented me a room next door. If you like, I can change in five minutes and take the children to the beach." Kiloa suggested.

"Would you guys like to go to the beach?" Manny asked. There were five happy cries for a trip to the beach.

"Well then, I suggest you all get your bathing suits on." Nicole smiled.

"Darn, I knew there was something I forgot to pack." Marsha frowned.

"No, you didn't mommy," Megan rebutted. "I watched you pack everything."

Marsha laughed, admitting that she was only teasing.

Kiloa excused herself and rushed off to her room to change for a day at the beach.

* * *

The next four days were spent basking in the sun and feasting at night. They were one big happy family. The kids grew to love their uncle Manny, but they simply adored their aunt Nicole. Marsha was elated to see her kids laughing and having so much fun after the death of their father. His death had been hard on them all. Still she cried every time she crawled into bed by herself. She missed Harold so much it hurt. She even missed his annoying snoring and cold feet.

Manny treated everyone to a Hawaiian pig roast. There were Hula girls wearing grass skirts with leis and flowers in their hair. Marsha and Nicole stepped in and tried to move their hips with the Hula girls, while Hawaiian men danced with sticks of fire. The dance was fast paced and electric, the kids especially loving the rhythm of the drums. Nicole and Marsha purchased a number of souvenirs. They bought grass skirts, leis, and flowers for their hair and right ankles.

After dinner, Manny asked Kiloa to watch the children and he escorted Marsha and Nicole to his suite. There was a table set with three glasses and a bottle of champagne on ice. Like the true gentleman he was, he pulled the chairs out and seated Marsha, then Nicole. Popping the cork on the bottle of champagne he filled three glasses.

"I would like to make a toast to the two most beautiful women in the world. Thank you both for bringing me so much happiness," Manny proposed.

They each held their glass high, clinked them together, and drank the sparking bubbly champagne. Nicole felt a tickle as she swallowed.

"I have one more surprise for you girls. Marsha, this is for your children." Manny handed her the information for five Trust Fund accounts, each worth fifty thousand dollars. "This is their college fund. If they choose not to go to college, their Trust will remain sealed until their twenty-fifth birthday. Hopefully, by then they will have learned to make better decisions."

For a moment Marsha stood there holding the documents in stunned silence. "I don't know what to say," she said, tears filling her eyes.

"Don't say anything," he smiled.

Nicole stood there looking happy for Marsha with a huge smile on her face. Manny reached into his light weight suit jacket pocket, and pulled out two long jewelry boxes.

"This is for the two loves of my life," he removed a diamond necklace from the first case and motioned for Nicole to let him slip it around her neck. Then a matching necklace went around Marsha's.

"Manny, this is too much. We can't accept all of this," Marsha said tearfully.

"Yes, you can. You have made an old man happy!"

Nicole yawned. "I'm so sorry! I'm tired."

"It's going to be a long trip home tomorrow," Marsha sighed.

"Well, why don't you girls get to bed early," Manny encouraged them. He kissed them both, bidding them a goodnight.

* * *

Manny undressed in preparation for bed. Grabbing the remote he turned on the television, and propped his feet up on the bed. He was proud of himself. It had been a great day and a marvelous vacation. He promised himself that next year he would surprise the girls with something even bigger and better.

Within five minutes of his watching the local news, he could hear a repeated knocking on the door of the suite. Manny stood up and slipping on a dressing gown, he left the bedroom to go answer the door. Nicole and Marsha burst into the room wearing grass skirts with flowered leis covering their bare breasts. They were barefooted with flower ankle bracelets on their right foot and a flower in their hair. They wiggled their hips and made motions with their hands.

"Aloha ha hee… Aloha ha hee," they sang moving their hips and making waving hand gestures.

Manny grinned from ear to ear and closed the door. The only clothing the girls had on was the grass skirts and leis. Beneath the grass skirt they were butt naked.

"This is for you, Manny!" Nicole announced, as she stripped away Marsha's grass skirt. Then Marsha stripped away Nicole's from her narrow hips, continuing to dance as they led Manny back into the bedroom.

Nicole kissed Marsha passionately while running her hands all over her body. From her soft full breast to the moistness of her mound. Nicole laid Marsha on top of the bed, spread her pussy lips and licked the juices from her. She got on her knees, unzipped Manny's pants and sucked his manhood while Marsha crawled between her legs to eat her pussy.

"Oh my God," Manny cried out a few moments later when he experienced the most intense orgasm in his entire life. Nicole was certainly his Honolulu baby. It was a time none of them would ever forget.

The next morning came all too quickly. Their departure flight was at nine fifteen in the morning. Marsha found that trying to pack, feed five children, and be ready to leave for the airport by eight a.m. was chaotic. Even with the help of the nanny, Kiloa, they rushed around in a frenzy barely making it to the airport on time.

After boarding the airplane and getting the kids settled into their seats, the flight went without any problems. The children sang songs and were well mannered.

Arriving back in Baltimore, Nicole said her good-byes and they parted company. She was scheduled to work at the Two O'Clock Club that night and it was already four o'clock in the afternoon.. Nicole picked up her luggage, then her car from long term parking, and drove home. She showered, dressed for work, and called Charlie to let him know she was back.

That night, when she went on stage, she showed off her dark tropical Hawaiian tan. After the club closed, she drove her Mercedes to the Wee Hours and parked behind Gus' red Malibu Super Sport convertible. When Stormy came in Nicole showed her and Gus all of the great photos she had taken in Honolulu.

At 3 a.m. Stormy left. As she was walking to her car, Domonic Coroza pulled up and parked behind her yellow Pontiac convertible. He honked, then motioned for Stormy to come talk with him. Domonic reached across the front seat of his Cadillac, smiled and opened the car door for her.

Stormy hesitated uncertainly before she sat down closing the door behind her. She immediately apologized profusely for her not keeping the appointment, explaining as he drove away that she failed to recall a family reunion in Kentucky. She reached inside her purse and returned his money.

As Nicole exited the Wee Hours, Stormy looked at her through the car window and waved.

Nicole smiled and waved back. She turned the alarm off on her Mercedes, unlocked the door, seated herself and keyed the ignition. A moment later she drove away giving Stormy a quick gesture with her hand indicating that she would call her later.

CHAPTER TWENTY-ONE
SOUNDS OF SILENCE

A single gunshot rang through the harbor, followed by a loud splash.

Carlos McConnell was working late, busy loading boxes onto a big cargo ship. It was hard to tell where the noise came from, the sound echoing across the harbor. He was sure what he heard was a gunshot and the splash following the sound horrified him, sending chills up and down his spine. Slowly he rubbed the goose bumps from his arms. This was his third year working the docks and he never heard or experienced anything like this before. His first instinct was to run, to hide, to get out of harms way. But like a statue he stood erect, listening to the stillness of the night while peering into the pitch black darkness for some type of movement, or sound, another gunshot, a scream, another splash, a footstep, a shadow, but there was nothing. Just the sound of silence.

Carlos looked at his watch, the time was three-thirty a.m. He pondered the thought of calling the police or emergency services. Except men on the docks were a different breed. If they wanted to keep their jobs, they learned to look the other way, to keep their mouths shut, and to mind their own business. Surely someone besides himself heard the shot, the sound having echoed around the harbor. Someone will report it, Carlos convinced himself as he picked up another box and carried it aboard the ship.

Another concerned citizen called the harbor police, reporting what looked like a body floating in the harbor off of pier five. A Coast Guard boat rushed to the scene and pulled a corpse from the dark water. The Baltimore Homicide detectives were quickly notified. Within fifteen minutes Detective Marks arrived on the scene. Over the past few months he had lost some twenty pounds, but he still looked like Jackie Gleason and puffed on the same smelly cigars.

"What do we have here?" Marks asked the Harbor Master.

"A female, twenty to thirty years of age. Brown hair, brown eyes. One shot to the head, right between her eyes."

Detective Marks placed a pair of latex gloves on his hands, and began searching the corpse's pockets. He found a Maryland Driver's license in the rear pocket of her jeans. The ambulance arrived, and Detective Marks released the dead body to the Coroner's office.

The morning news reported, "BALTIMORE KILLER AT LARGE.

This morning the harbor police recovered the body of Joyce Winland from the water off pier five. Authorities are seeking information anyone may have concerning this brutal murder. Contact Detective Marks at the Baltimore Homicide Division."

* * *

It was mid afternoon when Nicole called Stormy's house, and received no answer. She tried calling several times throughout the day, to no avail. Later that evening she parked her Bug in front of the Body Shop and went inside the bar. Chris was sitting on a barstool near the front door, so she sat down on a stool next to him.

"Is Stormy working tonight," she asked smiling.

Chris looked at her, with a sad look in his eyes. "Didn't you watch the news this morning?"

Nicole felt her stomach drop down to her knees, a sickening feeling in the pit of her stomach. "No, why?"

"The harbor police recovered the body of Joyce Winland from the harbor this morning. A serial killer may be on the loose."

"And?" Nicole asked dreading what his answer would be.

Chris looked at her with bloodshot eyes. His lower lip quivered as he said, "You dizzy bitch. You don't even know Stormy's real name, do you?"

Nicole's eyes filled with tears. She covered her face and said quietly, "I do now!"

"I just want to get my hands on the son of a bitch who killed her!"

Chris swore.

"I gotta go!" Nicole said and ran from the bar. She locked herself in her little yellow Volkswagen and wept uncontrollably. Gathering her thoughts, she started the car and drove to the Two o' Clock Club. Blaze was sitting in her normal place. Nicole sat down on a stool next to her.

"What's the matter honey?" Blaze asked, noticing the red in Peaches' eyes.

"Did you hear about the girl found in the harbor this morning?"

"Yeah."

"It was Stormy."

"It was Stormy?" Blaze repeated, sitting up straight. "Everyone is talking about it honey. There's a lot of concerned and upset people. It's bad for business! It wasn't reported to the police, but one of the workers on the dock heard a gunshot around three-thirty a.m."

"Three-thirty?" Nicole repeated, to make sure she heard Blaze correctly.

"Does that mean something to you?" Blaze asked.

"When I left the Wee Hours at three a.m. Stormy was sitting in Domonic Coroza's white Cadillac. A while ago he offered me three hundred dollars to do to a party and dance, but I was going to Hawaii, Stormy agreed to go. He paid her and as he was driving away she recalled that she had to go to a family reunion in Kentucky. She planned on giving him his money back when she saw him."

"Domonic Coroza. Crowbar? You do know that he's a hitman. He has well over thirty assaults on his record. He's served time for manslaughter and he's been found not guilty of two murders. You wouldn't know it to look at him. Just goes to show you, never judge a book by its cover."

"I gotta go!" Nicole suddenly stood up. After she left the club she immediately headed for the cabin in Pennsylvania to see Bulldog. After all, he was her protector. Her appearance was a surprise to him and what she had to tell him was enough to shock and anger him.

* * *

Early the next morning when Gus locked up the Wee Hours, he saw Stormy's Pontiac parked across the street. The car was completely covered in a thick layer of snow. He assumed her to have driven home with her friend Peaches.

The evening newspaper reported: 'MURDER AT THE HARBOR AND KILLER AT LARGE'. It was the second murder in a year. The murder of Sheila 'Missy' Watts was still unsolved. Dick and Jerry Everhart's girls were afraid to work the streets. When Jerry watched the evening news, he called Gus.

That night as Gus was turning the key in the door to open the after-hour club, he heard the roar of Harley engines. The Argots surrounded his and Stormy's car.

Bulldog got off his motorcycle and confronted Gus.

"Who are you?" Bulldog demanded.

"I own this place. My name is Gus Valakos. Is there a problem," he looked around at the many hard faced, bearded men, surrounding him.

"Is that Stormy's car." Bulldog pointed to the snow covered vehicle.

"I believe it is.'" Gus replied.

"She was fished out of the harbor this morning."

"I'm sorry, but l never knew Stormy's real name."

"My old lady was here with Stormy last night."

"Who's your old lady," Gus grinned.

"Peaches."

"Peaches?" Gus repeated in surprise, "She left right after Stormy around three a.m. Peaches showed me some photos she took vacationing in Honolulu."

"Honolulu?" Bulldog laughed, thinking how she had outsmarted him again. "The bitch told me she was going to visit her dying grandmother!"

"I could be mistaken." Gus chuckled.

"Peaches saw Stormy sitting in Domonic Coroza's white Cadillac at three a.m. A week ago Coroza gave her three hundred dollars to dance at his friend's birthday party. She accepted his money with every intention of dancing, but she forgot that she had to attend a family reunion in Kentucky. Peaches thinks she returned his money last night. She saw the two of them outside the Wee Hours at three a.m. The reported gunshot was heard in the harbor a half hour later. Do you know where Domonic lives?"

"No, I don't." Gus lied.

Bulldog handed Gus a card with his phone number at the cabin. "If you hear anything, call me. This is personal!"

* * *

Nicole went to see Manny. She told him about her friend Stormy, and he insisted on contacting her family on her behalf. Manny offered to pay for the funeral expenses, and make the arrangements, which they graciously accepted. Excluding family, the line to get in to pay their respects to Stormy was a half block long. More than a hundred Argots wearing their colors headed the procession, all of them there to support Nicole during her time of grief.

Manny offered a ten thousand reward for information leading to the arrest and conviction for the person or persons responsible for the murder of Joyce 'Stormy' Winland.

* * *

Gus called Jerry Everhart and asked him to call everyone in the loop. This included strip club owners, after-hour club owners, and a variety of other hustlers. If you ran an illegal dice game or the junket to Las Vegas you might be considered in the loop. A meeting was held at the Wee Hours at seven a.m., cars from the various participants lining Fleet Street. The owners were there to discuss the murders of Joyce 'Stormy' Winland and Sheila 'Missy' Watts.

Gus told his story about Missy's broken fingernails indicating a struggle had taken place during her murder. A day after her murder Domonic 'Crowbar' Coroza came into the Wee Hours with a band-aid across his face claiming he cut himself shaving. Then Gus told the story about Domonic paying Stormy three hundred dollars to dance at a friend's birthday party. About her last being seen sitting in his white Cadillac in front of the Wee Hours at three a .m. An unreported gunshot was heard in the harbor at three-thirty.

Everyone agreed that the evidence against Domonic was overwhelming and that something needed to be done. To add to that the Argots, an outlaw biker gang was looking for Domonic. Something needed to be done quickly. Everyone decided to contribute to the fund of getting rid of a troublesome problem, and a contract was issued on Domonic 'Crowbar' Coroza.

* * *

Domonic knew there was only one person who could link him to the murder of Stormy. It was the blonde little dancer, Peaches. For this reason he had been waiting for her to return home. On the first night of meeting her, he followed her home from the Blue Onion. Since that time he had stalked her with the intentions of snatching her one day. His killing of Stormy had derailed his previous plans, and now he must act quickly.

Fifteen minutes later Peaches parked and climbed out of the Mercedes, preparing to throw the car cover on for the night. It was after Two O'Clock in the morning and she was tired after putting in a long day's work. Before going to work she had completed a transaction between Charlie and the Argots attorney. She was just getting the cover pulled down over the Mercedes-Benz when she heard a scraping noise behind her. She spun around, to find herself face to face with the cold eyes of Domonic Coroza. Domonic grabbed her, spun her around, and covered her mouth with his hand.

"If you scream, bitch, I will kill you. Nod if you understand."

Peaches nodded.

As he removed his hand, she asked. "What do you want?"

"Shut up," he snapped, grabbing her by the arm. He walked her silently across the large parking structure to his car, opened the passenger door and ordered. "Get in!"

"Where are you taking me?"

"I thought you might want to see my place," he grinned.

From beneath his heavy winter coat he removed a snub nosed thirty-eight revolver letting her see it as he moved around to the driver side door, keeping the muzzle pointed in her direction the entire time. He climbed behind the driver seat and started the car.

"Why did you kill Stormy?" Nicole asked bluntly.

"When I pay someone to do something, I expect them to do it. She made me look bad!"

Nicole looked over to find his eyes looking wild with anger. She was too enraged herself to feel fear. This was the man possibly responsible for her daughter's death. This was certainly one way to find out.

"I know you beat Jeff Miles with a baseball bat."

Domonic looked at her hard and asked. "How do you know about that?"

"Tony told me," she lied.

"Doesn't surprise me. He had a big mouth."

"Did you kill Harold Bennett too?"

"Nah, Tony killed him. Then I killed Tony."

"Why?" Nicole asked, seeking to distract him as they drove along an icy street. Her biggest concern was the gun gripped in his left hand, which lay in his lap near the driver side door.

Domonic removed his right hand from the steering wheel for the split second it took to backhand her hard across the face. "Bitch, you ask too many questions."

Nicole's head slammed into the passenger side window. She turned sideways on the seat, tracking his every move and hating him with every fiber of her being. She wanted desperately to pound his head against the window.

He lived in a small two bedroom house in Essex. It was shingled white with a black roof and matching shutters. The backyard was fenced and two gates opened to the rear driveway. Domonic parked in front of the house, being careful to follow her out of the car through the passenger side door, the gun pressed hard in her back. He gave Nicole the keys to open the front door and escorted her inside. He shoved her through the house and upstairs to his bedroom where he handcuffed her to the cast iron frame of his bed.

"What are you going to do with me," she demanded.

"Whatever I want," he chuckled. He thought she was hot, and he wanted to have his way with her before he killed her.

"I'll give you a hundred thousand dollars if you let me go," she offered, hoping to prolong an attack she was sure would be coming quickly enough.

"Where would you get that kind of money?" Domonic laughed.

"I have it! It's in a shoe box under the bed at my apartment," she swore.

"If you're lying to me, I swear you will die a slow and painful death."

"I swear, I have the money. The key to my apartment is in my right front pocket."

As he searched her pocket for the key, a neighbor's dog started barking and continued to bark. Domonic went to look out the bedroom window over looking the front of the house. He saw nothing out of the ordinary. His Cadillac was still parked untouched at the curb. He smiled at Nicole before going to the bedroom closet for several coils of rope. He gagged her with a sock in her mouth and tied her feet using the rope. He walked out of the room assured that she would not be going anywhere soon. He went downstairs, stepped outside, and heard the roar of Harley motorcycles in the near distance.

He opened the driver's door of his car, sat down, inserted the key in the ignition and turned it. There was a 'click' and time seemed to slow in his mind's eye as the realization of the barking dog hit him. How many times in the past had he planted explosives in someone else's car. Before he could think further, there was a massive explosion. Upstairs in the house Nicole heard the explosion, followed by the rattling of the house windows.

Nicole heard sirens and it was another hour before the authorities got around to searching the house, where they discovered her gagged and handcuffed to the bed.

"Why were you handcuffed to the bed?" the police inquired.

"I don't know. I must have had too much to drink last night, and passed out," she lied.

"Do you live here?"

"No!"

"What can you tell me about the person who was blown up in the Cadillac out front?"

"Nothing!" Nicole said in pretended frustration.

"Do you know his name? How did you get here? Who handcuffed you to the bed? What's your name?" The young police officer asked one question after another,

"My name is Nicole Redman." That was the only question she answered.

She was taken to the police station for further questioning. "May I have a phone call, please." Nicole asked.

The officer working the desk handed her a phone, and she dialed Governor Marvin Mandell's phone number.

"Hello," he answered.

"This is Peaches. I need your help." She briefly explained the circumstances. He made one call, and ten minutes later she was released.

Nicole called Charlie for a ride.

"What happened?" Charlie asked, as they walked out of the police station.

"I don't want to talk about it." Nicole said, flatly. He dropped her off at the entrance of Regency Towers. Once inside, she asked the manager to unlock her door. She took a hot shower, then called a locksmith to change the locks.

* * *

Nicole opened the hall closet and grabbed a plastic baggy from her jacket. She laid out two lines of cocaine and snorted them while turning on the television. A news anchor for Channel seven reported, "Early this morning an explosion rocked the quiet neighborhood of Essex, the result of a car bombing leaving one man dead, Domonic Coroza. Coroza was believed to be a hitman with ties to organized crime."

* * *

Gus read about the explosion in the Baltimore Sun. When he went to open the Wee Hours that night he was met by a dozen Argots with their motorcycles parked at the curb.

"You lied to me, Gus. You knew where Domonic lived." Bulldog grinned.

"Like you said it was personal." Gus replied, hoping Bulldog would understand.

"I would have handled the problem for free. But now that I know about the fifty thousand dollar contract, I'm here to collect it. Don't play games with me!"

"How do I know you're responsible for what happened to Domonic?"

"There's nobody else claiming the friggin' reward, is there?"

"There's other people involved. I have to clear it with them."

"That's fine, but make sure you tell them that if I'm not paid, I will torture you until you give up their names. After I kill you, I will be to see them!"

The following morning Gus called the cabin and told Bulldog to come get his money.

* * *

Wednesday morning when Nicole went to Marsha's house she told her that Domonic 'Crowbar' Coroza was responsible for the death of her daughter Charlotte, Jeff Miles, Tony Bedsoe, and her friend Stormy.

"Tony Bedsoe, the manager of the Blue Onion, killed your husband Harold."

"Why?" Marsha asked tearfully.

"Domonic Coroza was a hitman. He has over thirty assaults on his criminal record and he was found not guilty of two murders he stood trial for. Tony acted as a middleman, setting the assault up. After Tony murdered Harold, Domonic killed Tony because the newspaper reported that he was cooperating with the police."

Bulldog was responsible for killing Domonic, but Nicole had no reason to share that information with anyone. Charlotte's murderer had been held accountable and by the grace of God her life had been spared.

Later that afternoon she and Marsha went to visit Manny. They entered the bedroom, closing the door behind them. Nicole would remain loyal to her dirty little family, with secrets.

DON'T MISS!

THE WEE HOURS PART II: PEACHES

BY W. D. BURNS

CHAPTER ONE
SNITCH ROAST

"The next time I tell you to steal a van, steal something worth stealing," Bulldog complained to Jammer. Bulldog was six-two, a solid two hundred and fifty pounds, with long brown hair and a full beard. His right hand man Jammer was an inch shorter with piercing blue eyes, long blonde hair and a thick beard. Five years earlier, when Bulldog was elected Sergeant of Arms for the Argot motorcycle club, the first member of Bulldog's crew was Jammer. He next picked Rooster, Cupcake, Kapote, and Tina to help him run security and protection for the outlaw club. Recently, J.D. became their newest prospect.

"It's rusty, but trusty," Jammer cracked.

The Ford van was white, rusty, leaking oil badly, and blowing clouds of smoke out of the exhaust. There was no time to argue, they were already at their destination. It was 4 a.m. and they had unfinished business to take care of.

Bulldog parked the van a few door down from the red brick rowhouse, located at 20 West Pratt street, grateful the six cylinder engine was at least quiet. They were less than ten blocks from the harbor, making the blowing wind bone chilling cold. As the crew quickly filed out of the van, crystals of snow danced around a street lamp at the corner. Turning their collars up to protect them from the bitter cold, they each grabbed their toboggan masks, and followed behind Tiny to the front door. While Bulldog looked up and down the street, the other men watched for any movement on the quiet street. A car, a person, a curtain suddenly opening, or a light coming on in a neighboring house. It took Tiny less than one minute to pick the Lock on the front door of the row-house, and even less time than that for them all to crowd silently inside, where they all covered their faces. A stairway to their right led to the upstairs bedrooms. Bulldog took the lead, creeping up the stairs, careful not to make any noise. The first bedroom was empty, but in the second Roger Pickett was curled up in a fetal position covered in a blanket. He was alone so they removed their masks. Cupcake, Tiny, and Rooster stood on one side of the bed, while Kapote, Jammer, and J.D. stood on the other side of the bed.

"Good morning!" Bulldog announced loudly, flipping a light switch to light up the room. Bulldog stood at the foot of the bed as a startled Roger Pickett popped up like a jack in the box. He looked around at the sight of the men surrounding the bed and his eyes went wide in terror. In a modest gesture he snatched up the blanket to cover himself. It was a pathetic sight, a reaction someone would anticipate coming from a girl.

"What do you want," he screeched in a high voice.

"You're not in a position to be asking questions. Don't talk, just listen. Follow my instructions and I promise that when we leave, which will be in about five minutes, you will be alive and unharmed. Nod if you understand?" Bulldog grinned.

Roger nodded, his eyes tearing.

"Lay down and stretch your arms out to the side of the bed." Roger complied. The prospect handed Jammer a rope from inside his jacket, and Bulldog instructed Jammer and Tiny to run the rope beneath the bed. Bulldog tied Roger's hands and feet tightly to the bed,

"I've got six hundred dollars in my wallet," Roger yelled.

Bulldog grabbed the pants draped across the back of a chair next to the bed, removed the wallet, and took the six hundred dollars. "Why thank you, Roger."

The men around the bed laughed. J.D. stepped forward, looked at the pathetic sight of Roger Pickett, and said, "Open wide!" As Roger opened his mouth J.D. jammed an apple in it, then wrapped binding tape around his head to hold the apple in place.

Bulldog took a knife from his pocket, bared two wires and connected them. He placed a chair next to the bed, set a timer for five minutes, then placed the bare wires in a pile of gunpowder. When the timer went off, it would create a huge spark.

"Do you remember your old friend, Charlie? Charlie Redman, the guy you grew up with. The two of you went to grade school together. The guy who sold you cocaine, and the guy you set up for the police. Well my friend, we are here to insure that it doesn't happen a second time. Charlie has such a forgiving nature. Unfortunately for you, I don't. And when you fuck over one of us, you fuck over all of us. However, I always keep my promises. I promised that when we left you would be alive and unharmed." After saying this, Bulldog doused Roger from head to toe with a gallon of camper fuel. "We're leaving now," Bulldog whispered with a smile.

Roger was already crying and struggling to free himself from his bonds, muffled sounds escaping from around the apple in his mouth. The crew locked the door behind them as they exited the row-house. They sat in the van with the engine running. Bulldog rolled a joint, lit it, and passed it around. When they saw flames coming from the upstairs bedroom, Bulldog drove away…

ABOUT THE AUTHOR

William Daniel Burns was born in Lakeland, Florida. His family, and those who knew him in his early years called him "Danny." At an early age, he discovered his gift for conning people to get whatever he wanted. At the age of five, he convinced his best friend that two rusty nails and a piece of wood were from George 'Washington's rocking chair and they would someday be worth a whole lot more then his old shiny silver dollar.

When he was seven, his father moved the family to Baltimore, MD. It was a much tougher neighborhood. Danny learned to fight, and hustle. His parents divorced when he was twelve. His younger sister and older brother chose to stay with his mother. Danny chose to live with his father. They returned to live in Florida., and Danny changed his name to "Bill." His father remarried when he was thirteen. Bill quit school, and left home when he was fifteen. He married, and had two beautiful daughters by the age of seventeen - Tina Marie, and Kerri Ann. He was ill-prepared to handle the responsibility, and moved back to the mean streets of Baltimore, where he turned to crime as a means to support his family. The police made a game of that by telling him they rode around in marked cars and wore uniforms, then asked what does a criminal look like. Bill purchased a yellow panel truck and wrote THIEF WAGON across the back and sides in big black bold letters. The game ended with Bill being sent to prison.

Released from prison, he found his wife remarried and his daughters calling another man "daddy." Bill felt that he had nothing left to lose and devoted his life to crime!

Bill returned to federal prison twice. He furthered his education by obtaining his G.E.D., a degree in Commercial Art, and he has the equivalent of a two-year college Associates Degree. Bill has owned a number of successful businesses.

In 1988, Bill worked as an independent contractor for O's Auto Sales in Walbridge, Ohio. In 1991, while the owner vacationed in Florida, Bill was left in charge of the business. Several other guys also used the license, but they weren't registered to buy or sell vehicles at the auctions.

On May 29, 1991 Bill left with his girlfriend on a Florida vacation, returning June 8, 1991. A fire occurred at Adrian Auto Auction May 31, 1991, and a murder occurred in Northwood, OH on June 7, 1991. When questioned in regard to the murder, Bill accounted for his whereabouts for the entire vacation.

In 1993 Bill was charged with stolen vehicles in Monroe and Adrian, Michigan.

On the advice of two attorneys Bill pled guilty. At sentencing, he told the judge there was nothing anyone could do when they are signed, sealed, and delivered. That just because he signed the titles, it did not necessarily mean the vehicles were his!

Bill served his sentence, and in 1998, he was transferred to the halfway House in Monroe, Michigan. Ten days before his release, he was charged for the arson of Adrian Auto Auction. The prosecutor contended that his motive for the arson was to destroy incriminating evidence, the titles to the stolen vehicles. Bill filed three formal motions for discovery - none were complied with! He refused plea offers of 10 years, 5 years, and 2 years with credit for six months served. Bill was convicted, and sentenced to serve LIFE. He still maintains his innocence.

Bill is a strong supporter of prison reform. He wants to let the youth of today know that crime, drugs, and violence is not a "game." Bill thanks God for his love, insight, and guidance as he journeys through life. For more information on him, please contact him via www.jpay.com. He is inmate number #189577.

ORDER MORE EXCITING NOVELS FROM W.D. BURNS!

Bad Ass Outlaw Publications

Mail:

Bad Ass Outlaw Publications
4216 Riverviwe Lane
Lorian, OH 44055

Name: _____

Address:_____

City/State:_____

Zip:_____

Quantity	Titles	Price	Total
_____	The Wee Hours	$12.95	____
_____	The Wee Hours II: Peaches	$12.95	____
_____	The Wee Hours III: Florida Snow	$12.95	____

Add $3.95 for shipping and handling (Via Priority Mail) for
1 book, $5.95 for 2 books , $8.95 for 3-4 books, add $1.95
for each additional book.

Total: $_____

FORMS OF ACCEPTED PAYMENT: Certified or government
issued checks and Money Order, all mail in order takes 7-10
Business Days to be delivered.

Or, just order online at http://www.badassoutlawpublications.com!

www.ingramcontent.com/pod-product-compliance
Lightning Source LLC
Chambersburg PA
CBHW072053170626

46813CB00004B/1330